Conquering Berlin
Wilfrid Bade

DIE SA EROBERT BERLIN

CONQUERING BERLIN

BY

WILFRID BADE

TRANSLATED BY THEODOR RUNEN

ANTELOPE HILL PUBLISHING

Der SA gewidmet!

Dedicated to the SA!

Contents

Translator's

Foreword

"History is written by the victors." A phrase uttered by many, hinting at a kernel of truth. And despite all of its shortcomings, this short sentence affords an interesting perspective on the book at hand.

At first glance, *Conquering Berlin* appears as a clear attempt to write history from the winning side, claiming seven years of political struggle in the German capital for the National Socialist movement and its paramilitary organization, the Sturmabteilung (SA). Originally published in 1933, the year of the final National Socialist election victories, the book was written by an ambitious young staff member in the newly founded Reich Propaganda Ministry, who also appears as the author of a short Joseph Goebbels biography, published in the same year. The book would go on to become a moderate success, reaching its eighth edition in 1943. For many a contemporary observer, this should suffice to condemn the notion of Bade's novel as a pure propaganda piece, a mere cash-in on a political victory, no longer of interest to the modern reader.

But while *Conquering Berlin* is clearly associated with the politics of the propaganda ministry, it still offers a relevant view into the daily life of the interwar period in Germany, its colloquial ductus covering layers of meaning and insight all but lost to modern historians. Bade's narrative exhibits a clear focus on the years of 1926–1930, the "fighting years" of the movement, when the NSDAP's success was still far from certain. This is particularly true for Berlin, a left-wing stronghold with one of the lowest electoral outcomes for the National Socialists in the entire Reich throughout the final years of the Weimar Republic. In this urban environment dominated by hostile left-wing paramilitary groups and an establishment police force, provocative campaigns by the newly appointed *Gauleiter* (a regional party leader) Joseph Goebbels were bound to create not only attention, but friction as well. This friction would lead to a multitude of clashes between SA, other political paramilitaries, and the police, frequently claiming lives on all sides.

Chronically underfunded, repeatedly outlawed, and under constant physical attacks by left-wing groups, the "conquest" of Berlin is portrayed as an arduous struggle by working-class or unemployed men for visibility, support of the local populace, and, most importantly, against violent crowds of communist thugs. This is in remarkable contrast to modern renditions, which tend to cast SA men as violent brutes, while giving their left-wing counterparts that unmistakeable halo of the heroic revolutionary.

Although its original German title *Die SA erobert Berlin: Ein Tatsachenbericht* (*The SA conquers Berlin: A factual report*) might suggest otherwise, *Conquering Berlin* is clearly a piece of historical fiction. It is highly unlikely that Bade himself took part in the street fights—while he did join the NSDAP in 1930, he was never a member of the SA, nor a particularly good fit for its target demographic of the unemployed, working-class, and veterans as Bade was working as a journalist after university studies in history and politics. However, it is entirely reasonable to assume that he had direct access to SA men with first-hand experience of SA activities during the late 1920s and early 1930s. In fact, many of the events recounted within this novel did take place, such as the incidents at the Lichterfelde train station, protest actions against *All Quiet on the Western Front,* or the various brawls in assembly halls.

But while these occurrences are well-documented in police reports and other documents, *Conquering Berlin* introduces the reader to a relatively unique perspective, generally favorable to the National Socialist and SA side of things. Considering this perspective is vital, as no truly objective sources on these events are widely available today. The degree to which hostile political and establishment sources can twist a narrative should be well known to the twenty-first century reader. As such, the only way we can try to approach an "objective" reading of history is by comparing multiple perspectives, both against each other and against our own experiences. *Conquering Berlin* offers the other end of the spectrum, a counterweight against mainstream historical and political narratives, helping us to sound the misty depths of the past.

Perhaps history really is written by the victors. But as the short-lived German National Socialist experiment shows us, victory itself

can be fleeting. Yesterday's victors may easily turn into tomorrow's
vanquished. History can always be reconquered.

Theodor Runen
March 2nd, 2021

1

STROLL

The worker Schulz slowly strolls through Potsdamer Straße. He doesn't care much for strolling, and he isn't particularly fond of Potsdamer Straße either—he might just as well go for a walk somewhere else. It's lunchtime on a warm autumn day, but he doesn't care much about that either, except that he's glad he can still walk without a coat. Because the worker Schulz doesn't own a coat. Matter of fact, he doesn't own anything at all, because he has been out of work for a long while.

So he has an infinite amount of time.

He can get up when he wants and sleep when it suits him. He has time to wait around at the unemployment office, he has enough time to listen to the endless debates going on there, and he has plenty of time to think about everything he hears in those debates.

He is a thoughtful person and by no means stupid. On his long walks he thinks about everything he sees and hears. He looks at the shops with their splendid displays of things which he never has been and never will be able to buy.

This does not upset him. The only time he becomes slightly disgruntled is when he takes a relaxed look at the posh, luxurious places where already at this time of day certain figures are sitting about, figures who make him sick to his stomach. He never cared about the Jewish question, not a bit. But he cannot help but notice a bad feeling rising up in him when he sees these faces, many of which are Jewish. He can't explain this feeling to himself, and he doesn't want to anyway. He can't stand these people, and that's that.

Close to his sleeping spot in Zoffenerstraße there is a strange place, a secretive pub that is crawling with this kind at night.

Without meaning to, he has acquired a lot of knowledge about such places on his walks, but it has not yet crossed his mind to get furious about them.

Sometimes he modestly thinks that he should really be entitled to some kind of work at least. Those three years on the Western front, he thinks, might have given him that right. He hadn't exactly been a big shot there, but if a superior had told him to go somewhere, he had gone there, and if another had told him to hold a position, he had held that position. Like many hundreds of thousands of others, he had been a simple, obedient, and faithful soldier, he had received his two wounds and recovered, and again he went into battle, humble, obedient, and faithful—but all that was over and forgotten. Probably the whole world had forgotten about it, and so there was no point in dwelling on it any longer.

Now he strolls across the Potsdam Bridge. Here is another one of those strange places. Schulz knows its particular secret. At this time of day it is a solid, middle-class inn where one can have an entirely decent lunch for one mark and fifty pfennig. *But* if you have enough money and want to have a good time, you can also go there after ten o'clock in the evening to drink and eat and also buy some cocaine if you are so inclined—because this is a headquarters of the Berlin coke dealer association.

The worker Schulz has no idea how much fun he could have snorting coke. But even if he only wanted to go there in the evening to have a glass of wine, they wouldn't let him in. Impossible! Dear God! A man in battered, striped black trousers, a cheap green shirt and an old leather jacket? Such a guest would not even make it to the door. Nah, that's nothing for his kind. At best, his kind is allowed to play lookout if the gentlemen do not want to be disturbed.

Oh dammit, thinks Schulz bitterly, *it's all such nonsense!* What kind of a republic is this anyway? Black, red, and gold and freedom, huh? So what was that revolution all about back then? About the worker, dear Schulz, wasn't it?

Of course, Schulz thinks, *and that's why I now have so much time to stroll through Berlin.* It's been a quarter year now. Schulz reaches for the last cigarette butt in his breast pocket. He doesn't have a lighter. What does he have anyway, honestly? And somewhat resignedly he stops a man coming towards him.

"Hello, comrade. Can I have a light?" Schulz asks as he looks into two strangely bright grey eyes.

"Sure," says the other. "You're smoking butts. Unemployed, eh?"

"Obviously," Schulz replied uninterested.

"You saying you're not? On the dole as well, huh?"

Meanwhile Schulz holds his poor stub to the other man's burning cigarette.

Slowly, Grey Eyes asks, "You're not doing anything else tonight, are you?"

"No," replies Schulz in surprise, feeling strange. "No, I don't have anything planned. Why?"

The other one takes the stump out of Schulz's mouth, reaches into his pocket and offers him a package. "Have a whole one for a change. Butts don't taste too good."

Schulz grabs it in surprise, quickly rolling the cigarette between his fingers for a quick assessment. Sixers! Six-Pfennig cigarettes! That's something. The boy must be doing well.

"Well," Grey Eyes slowly repeats, "if you're not going anywhere, you can tag along."

Schulz has become suspicious. "Where to?" he asks somewhat brusquely. Who does that guy think he is to just ask him? He does not like that kind of thing. Unsure, the worker Schulz keeps turning the expensive cigarette between his fingers.

"Don't worry about the cigarette," Grey Eyes explains with a smile. "They're from my old man. He owns a coal shop and I took that box for the PCs. He won't mind."

"PC?" Schulz asks, purely out of politeness because of the free cigarette. "PC? What's that? Some kind of new thing?" He looks the man straight in the face.

He answers calmly, "PC is short for Party Comrade, and the whole thing is called NSDAP, meaning National Socialist German Workers' Party. And that's a good thing; you can count on that."

The worker Schulz grins fiercely. "Workers' Party? Sounds like we got a big shot here! Workers' Party is a good one, man. I can't stand that stuff. No, sir, I've had enough of the SPD.[1] Way too many Workers' Parties and no work! I always hear them going on about Workers' Parties! It is a party for workers, correct? So what have they done for the workers? Nothing, my good man. You have done nothing at all. We go on the dole, we have nothing to eat, nothing to wear, nowhere to stay—"

---

[1] The Social Democratic Party of Germany (SPD, *Sozialdemokratische Partei Deutschlands*), a moderate/reformist Marxist political party chiefly responsible for the creation of the Weimar Republic and which remained the largest party in the *Reichstag* until 1932.

And then Schulz suddenly reflects, his eyebrows raising themselves high on his forehead. "Oh, man... Right... Now I remember. You are the fascists, right? Nah... You're not workers at all... Man, just wait until us workers really get going..."

Grey Eyes calmly lets him finish his thought, looking at him attentively in the meantime. Now he speaks in his slow, insistent way, "You're the real deal, I can see that. Once you workers get to marching, you say? Didn't you march in 1918?[2] Well? Of course you did! And what did you accomplish? You tore away the officer's epaulets and that felt great to you, didn't it? And you made a great racket everywhere, imagining that you had killed everything that was rotten, didn't you? Good heavens, but who did you actually get rid of? The capitalists? Nope! The Jews? No! The exploiter? No, no. So what? You got a job now? No! You don't even have a cigarette. What do you have anyway? Where is the peace? Where's the Rhineland? Where is Upper Silesia? Do you know what you've got? You got the corridor and tributes and you still have the capitalists."

Schulz is speechless. "Gently, gently," he growls excitedly. "That's too fierce. Now I get it. You're a right-winger! Don't act all high and mighty. So what have you done? A coup with generals, the Reichswehr[3] and all of that nonsense. Screw yourself, man! Did that do any good? No. Let me tell you something. I know all about it. The worker today, he's no longer human. If you're tired of him, you can just throw him out. If your profits start to dwindle, what do you do? Just kick the worker out, then you don't have to pay him a salary. The farmer is taken care of. He won't starve. He's always got potatoes and a bit of bread. Definitely. He always has something to chew on. But all us workers have is a hand on our necks, holding us up above the abyss. And we can't do anything. If it suits the hand, it lets go. Then we get drowned, right into the abyss, and the infighting starts. That's the way it is, and you won't change that with a coup.

"We have to bring about something completely different. That hand has to come off. We workers have to be grounded somewhere instead of always hovering over the abyss, you know? But you can't do that with parties. That is education. The worker is a human being too.

---

[2] This refers to the German "November Revolution" near the end of the First World War and its immediate aftermath, initially sparked by a sailors' revolt in Kiel during late October and early November, which led to the abdication of the Kaiser and the creation of the Weimar Republic.
[3] The armed forces of the Weimar Republic.

He's not supposed to be that prole, which the lofty citizens make him out to be. He is just as important as them. Work does not defile. Nonsense, it certainly defiles when it is for those bourgeois gentlemen. And as long as that hasn't ended, hasn't changed, your parties can bite me."

The other one has continued to give the angry man his calm and attentive looks. Now he hands him the whole packet. "Here. Take this. And I want to tell you one more thing: Why in God's name don't you do something about it yourself?"

And with that, Grey Eyes calmly continues down the street, leaving the worker Schulz to his problems. Schulz feels like he just got punched right in the gut. Somewhat stunned, he walks on, absently looking at the shop windows every now and then, but neither his eyes nor his heart are really in it.

Then suddenly he growls to himself, "Why don't you do something about it?"

He is thinking hard about it.

*　*　*

Grey Eyes has disappeared into the entrance of an old, dark house on Potsdamer Straße.

He walks quickly across the courtyard, his eyebrows tightly drawn together, until he turns left into an entrance that looks like the mouth of a cave. A sign reads:

NSDAP Berlin—Branch Office.

He enters a truly gloomy room. Plaster is coming off the walls, and there is an off mix of smells—dust, sweat, and cold beer. The office is made up of two rooms. Each room contains a table and a few chairs. The tables are littered with papers and sandwiches.

There is an old, half-opened cabinet, a scraped brown shirt hanging about, a file folder lying on the floor with a pair of army boots next to it. A revolver is resting peacefully on a chair right next to a worn, bitten pen.

In the back room Grey Eyes hears three people arguing. He smiles to himself, a tired little smile. Actually, why shouldn't the three of them argue, he thinks, when the entire leadership of the Berlin NSDAP section is at loggerheads?

He stops for a little while and listens to the noise. The bare walls give their echoing voices a strangely hollow sound. And all at once, Grey Eyes remembers that scene from a patrol at Col di Lana,[4] when the German and Austrian NCOs argued about which way to go. Back then, the voices had sounded just as hollow—until the stress had come to a radical close, when the Italians ended the dispute by shooting down both the German and the Austrian NCO. And it will be similar here, Grey Eyes thinks, very similar indeed, unless...

And suddenly he rushes into the next room.

His voice is no longer as slow and quiet, as it was during his encounter with the unknown worker earlier; it has become fast, sharp, and flaming.

"Shut it!" he says. "I want to tell you something. Now, whoever of you is more or less important, I don't care. But it's pretty apparent that none of you is a real National Socialist. And that this whole place is a pigsty, I know that too. What are you doing, what are you actually doing?"

It has become quiet in both rooms, and people look at him, concerned and angry. As he continues, his voice is hoarse with suppressed anger. "What are you doing?" he snarls at them. "Why do you gather here? Do you hold meetings so that Berlin at least knows you exist? No! Do you care about what our other party comrades are doing? No! Have you ever even brought a single new person here? No! Do you have decent accounting and treasury? No! What do you call this dump? An office? No, thank you!"

He has stepped up close to them, his grey eyes dark with outrage. "And I want to tell you another thing," he growls between his teeth. "If you go on like this, I'm going to take three SA-Men, occupy this dump, and close it down. I get sick just looking at you. Outside on the street the most magnificent material is running around, people we can use, SA-Men who just don't know it yet, future National Socialists, and none of you are going out to look for them! And why not? Because all of you want to play the leader instead of doing the actual work! You dream of great stories, but you have to start with the little ones, or it will never work. You have to catch people! But this stops now, I can assure you! One way or another! We will have order here, and I'm going to tell you who is going to bring it. Not me and not you either,

---

[4] Col di Lana is a mountain in the Italian Dolomites that saw some intense fighting in the First World War, primarily between Austrian and Italian troops.

but Dr. Joseph Goebbels. You ought to be familiar with that name."

And with that, Grey Eyes tears the old brown shirt from its cabinet, slams the door behind him and storms out into the courtyard, almost knocking over a man who is carefully studying the office sign.

"Oops," says the man.

"Sorry," mumbles Grey Eyes, before he suddenly stops and stares at the man, who grins at him happily.

"May I? Schulz!" he says. "I've already had the honor. You're all just big shots here, aren't you? I've been listening. No, I don't think this is going to work out. I'm off." But just as he turns to leave, he is twisted around by his shoulders.

"Look at this," says Grey Eyes very gently. "This is a brown shirt. And you'll be wearing one of these in four weeks, as sure as my name is Karl and I'm an SA-Man."

And with that he disappears for the second time today, leaving behind a concerned and thoughtful worker Schulz.

* * *

With his endless amount of time, the worker Schulz slowly drifts homewards, through Potsdamer Straße towards Schöneberg, through Bülowstraße and Yorckstraße, but then he ends up back in the pub at Zossener Straße again.

He doesn't care much for pubs, but how else is he supposed to spend the long evening? Besides, he always manages to find some interesting people in this pub.

KPD[5] is written above the door, and inside, above the round corner table, hangs the Soviet star.

Schulz walks up to the bar and orders a pint, listening to what the interesting people at the corner table are talking about. They discuss everything very openly and seem to have no secrets at all.

"23 reported it," one of them says, making the others nod and grin.

"What's his name?" asks one of them.

"Goebbels," replies another, and the worker Schulz pricks up his ears. He has heard this name before—earlier today, when he stood in front of the NSDAP office.

And because Schulz knows one of the men at the corner table, he

---

[5] The Communist Party of Germany (KPD, *Kommunistische Partei Deutschlands*), founded in late 1918 by Rosa Luxemburg and Karl Liebknecht.

goes and sits down with a short greeting. He is always curious about what is going on in the world.

"Goebbels?" he asks. "What about him? Who is that?"

An acquaintance laughs. "Who is that? That is the new Berlin *Gauleiter*[6] for the Nazis. He raised a big fuss in the Ruhr and now they want him to turn around things here. He needs to watch out. Berlin is red and it remains red. And anyone who stands up against the Commune gets knocked down. Even Mr. Goebbels."

"Well, well," says Schulz thoughtfully. "You don't seem too fond of that guy."

"You can bet on that. He won't do any meetings here! Not here! Maybe in Spandau, they got a few Nazis sitting out there. But here, never!"

"They have an office in Potsdamer Straße, don't they?" Schulz asks cautiously. The men at the table look at each other and start guffawing. "That dump?" someone asks dismissively. "Not worth our time. Nah, we've got better things to do. Isn't that right, Gustav?" They exchange meaningful looks again and wink at each other.

And then they tell their old stories again about the glory of the Soviets and all the things that have to be changed in these German lands, all the things that have to be turned completely upside down, and the worker Schulz can feel his mood deteriorating even further.

It's all a big pile of crap, he thinks bitterly as he gets up and leaves, *one big dung heap.*

He hurries to get some fresh air, almost stumbles out of the pub, and bumps into a fat man who loses his balance a little.

"Oh," Schulz says startled and holds the fat man by the arm so he can catch himself and get back up.

But the fat man, who is well dressed and emits a remarkable odor of beer, furiously tears himself away. He looks the worker Schulz up and down—his poor trousers, his cheap green shirt and the worn leather jacket—and yells at him, "Watch what you're doing you dirty prole!"

This horrible word hits the worker Schulz like a hot, devouring flame; he can no longer bear this terrible word.

His fist flies right into the fat man's face, making him stagger, and

---

[6] The National Socialists organized Germany into a number of districts called *Gauen*, regional areas under the leadership of a *Gauleiter*, a designated official who held overall responsibilities for the regional party organization.

then Schulz slams left and right into this fat face until he sinks to the ground wailing.

People are gathering around him, and a policeman arrives. The worker Schulz has stopped calmly. He cannot quite decide whether to be surprised at himself. It had to happen at some point. The pent-up rage had to overflow.

With a painful grip, the policeman takes Schulz by the upper arm and leads him to the station. Children run after them.

Schulz is very familiar with this spectacle: a badly dressed man under the fist of a policeman. The thought that he is now personally involved in this scenario almost makes him smile.

At the police station the constable looks him over at the gate, a short glance from below.

"Got a party?" he asks.

The worker Schulz is about to shake his head when he is seized by a strange feeling hitherto unknown, a feeling composed of defiance, longing, homesickness, anger, disappointment...

"Nazi," he says aloud.

"Oh, I see," says the policeman who brought him there, and before the worker Schulz can figure out what this "Oh, I see" means, he is hit right over the head with a rubber truncheon.

*Red Front! This is what Berlin looked like in 1927, when Dr.
Goebbels accepted the Gauleiter position. Pictured is a mass assembly
of the Red Front Fighters Association.*

Gauleiter Dr. Joseph Goebbels addresses the SA.

2

ARRIVAL

It has become late autumn and temperatures are dropping. There has already been a little snow, but now the rain and clouds have returned.

In the two rooms at Potsdamer Straße the few National Socialists are sitting together, and they are not exactly having a good time. It is November 9th and they are mourning doubly. First, for November 9th, 1918, the day on which a hard-working, brave and patient people were beaten to the ground, and also for November 9th, 1923, which they call the day of betrayal.[7] Berlin is flying all red flags, and the city's hundred proud SA-Men walk beneath these flags with a bitter heart.

A quiet restlessness can be felt in the office. People put their heads together and whisper.

Grey Eyes smiles to himself as he throws around a few secret glances every now and then. There they are sitting, the ambitious, the schemers, troublemakers, agitators, the dissatisfied and self-proclaimed leaders, and all of them have become a little quieter.

This evening, Dr. Joseph Goebbels is due to arrive in Berlin.

Grey Eyes is daydreaming about how things will change now. Will this gigantic field, this colossus, this immense accumulation of people, views, and convictions, will Berlin be conquered or not? It is the most difficult task a man could be given, an almost superhuman task.

Karl is dreaming, and with his entire, hot heart he is drawn towards this man who is on his way to help them. If he isn't a fighter, thinks Karl, gritting his teeth, if he is not a fighter without fear and reproach, if his is not a fist made of iron, a head clever as a snake, and a heart as hot as a flame, then Berlin will never be within their grasp,

---

[7] November 9th, 1923 was the date of Hitler's first attempt to gain power during the failed Munich Beer Hall Putsch, which was betrayed by several Bavarian government officials.

but lost for all time. Because it is almost too late.

Towards evening Karl grabs his two friends Kurt and Max. "Let's go," he says somewhat depressed, "to the station. If we're going to get a new Gauleiter, we might as well have a look at him."

The three SA people pack up, leaving behind quite a mess. The cashier is sitting over his books, his head smoldering like a chimney. He calculates and calculates until he finally gets tired of it. Looking around, he notices that nobody else is around anymore, so he takes his cap, puts the books in some corner, and leaves. The two dark rooms of the office are now desolate, cold and hopeless.

At the Friedrichstraße station, six calm, incorruptible, and inquisitive worker eyes rest on a small, dark-haired man who has just got off the train and is looking around. Karl walks up to him. "You are Dr. Goebbels?"

And in the two seconds between question and answer, Grey Eyes examines the new Gauleiter with a searching gaze and an open heart. His face is gaunt and sharp, his movements are energetic, he carries his head high, but his clothes are poor, just like theirs. Even though they are much taller than him, they fall for the man right away. His large eyes, clear and pure, look into theirs, they do not shy away, and there is something special that captures them: this wonderful, light smile, radiant and boyish, with which he greets them.

All right, thinks Karl, and without him being able to explain it, an unprecedented feeling of happiness flows through him, *all right.*

"We are," he begins, "we are from the SA and welcome you to Berlin."

Dr. Goebbels looks at the three from his calm eyes. "You will have to fight," he says.

And Karl exclaims, "If we can do that, Doctor, we will have Berlin. You can count on us."

Dr. Goebbels breathes a sigh of relief. "Well..." he says.

"Yes, sir!" the three answer and now the new Gauleiter smiles and his eyes sparkle at them.

"There's a meeting in District 2 today," Karl says as they walk down the steps. "November 9th and all that."

"That's where we're going," says Goebbels immediately, "by bus if we can. I want to see Berlin."

Above his head, the three SA-Men exchange some happy and surprised looks. And Karl thinks, *this is the fighter, the head and the heart.* So everything is fine.

"Do you already have a place to stay?" Kurt asks.

The Doctor waves the question away. "Another time. I'd rather hear about the meeting. How big is the hall? How many people visit? How many do you think are there today? Where is the hall? What's that whole area like?"

The three of them are taken aback. Good Lord, why does he want to know all this? Are they supposed to know all that? They have to admit that they never bothered with such details, but they try to answer his questions from memory nevertheless. Then the Doctor inquires about the Berlin NSDAP, and here the three of them have no need to strain their memories. They know enough about that topic, way more than they would like to, actually.

Two hours after his arrival, the new Gauleiter speaks to the Berlin Party comrades, and the Berlin Party is stunned. They haven't heard that kind of talk before! It sweeps over them like a roller-coaster. One minute they feel crushed and defeated, the next one they proudly raise their heads sky-high. Oppressing and uplifting at once, he reaches directly into their hearts and fills their minds with singular determination.

Karl and his two friends hardly dare to catch their breath. *Now everything will be all right,* he thinks. But at first it seems as if things are still far from all right. The public echo is very poor.

A single Jewish newspaper reports maliciously: "A certain Mr. Goebbels, it is said he comes from the Rhineland, produced himself and tapped into the familiar old phrases." That was all.

What does the NSDAP mean to Berlin anyway? It was a crude, confused bunch—a few hundred people, each of them with his own particular brand of National Socialism.

Should one even deal with such a bunch?

Berlin says no.

The SA says yes.

And the SA takes up the challenge.

In their midst now stands a man by the name of Dr. Joseph Goebbels, and this man hammers the party program into the hearts and minds and every thought of the SA.

"We are six hundred people in Berlin," he hammers, "in six years, we must be 600,000! You have to fight, fight incessantly. The SA is the party's elite; the SA-Man is the first political soldier in Germany. The movement is unknown in this city; it is ridiculed, in the dark. It must emerge from this darkness. One shall take notice of it! They will insult us, slander us, fight us, beat us to death—they shall do all of this—but they will speak of us. Today, our fight begins. SA of Berlin, our watchword is: *Attack!!!*"

3

Loss

The attack has begun. And the Commune notices its onset. They double their informers, and these informers are everywhere. No. 23 has given an excellent report. No. 311 reports further.

No. 311 also reports on the construction worker Kurt Tennigkeit, an SA-Man who once had a conversation with Dr. Joseph Goebbels.

Kurt Tennigkeit works on scaffolding near Weissensee.

One day his foreman Henkel climbs up to him. Foreman Henkel, a man with fists like two children's heads, is a Red Front man[8] of the highest degree.

Henkel, fists in his trouser pockets, watches the boy work for a while. Then he says, "Well, found something?"

Tennigkeit raises himself up and looks into the brutal face of the foreman. He stops and thinks: *Caution.*

They are three stories above ground, and the scaffolding is only three feet wide. "Found something? What do you mean?"

Henkel steps closer, close to the boy. "You don't know? Something to help you with the bootlicking. I wanna tell you something: We don't need fascists here, get it? This isn't the spot for your propaganda, get it? I do propaganda here and no one else. Not even your labor-murderer Goebbels. So get lost, my boy, you don't belong with us honest proletarians. Hurry up and get lost!"

The boy hasn't flinched, not a single step. Calmly, he looks the older man in the eyes. "I'm a worker just like you," he says bravely, "I can work wherever I want, and if you've got a problem with that..."

Foreman Henkel's face turns cherry-red, and he slowly pulls his

---

[8] The *Roter Frontkämpferbund* (literally, "Red Front Fighters Association") was a paramilitary organization associated with the Communist Party of Germany during the Weimar Republic.

hands out of his pockets.

"Oh yeah? Oh yeah?" he growls, an evil light flickering in his eyes, "You want to threaten me, you lout? Are you threatening me? Have a look down there! You in for a little crash, eh? Your cabbage head always seemed rotten to me, you fascist pig!"

The world suddenly turns black before SA-Man Tennigkeit's eyes. What did the Doctor say? "They're going to insult us and fight us..."

The young man doesn't think of allowing them to insult the party, the Doctor, and himself. He slowly takes a step back, away from the abyss, and then he swings his fists, hitting Henkel right in the face.

And with a single leap, he is at the ladder. He has learned to climb ladders; like a weasel he sweeps down the rungs, and for the moment, he is happy. He has been brave; he stood his ground.

At the top he hears Henkel roaring, and the whole construction site answers him. Suddenly a raging hatred breaks out behind the walls, on the ladders, around the whole scaffolding.

"Bricks!!!" someone yells.

"Bricks!" it roars from all sides, from above and below. The Commune rises. *Yes, bricks!* thinks Tennigkeit as he sweeps further down, rejoicing in his own speed and agility.

But then, as the bricks whiz around his ears from all sides, he realizes that he is climbing for his life. And when he is still thirty feet above ground and looks down, he knows that he is lost. Some of them are already down there and their faces are cold and pale with steaming rage.

With a bold leap, the young SA-Man jumps into their midst. There is no point in running anymore. One of them lifts a crowbar and hits him over the head with it. The worker Kurt Tennigkeit sinks into a black abyss, a thundering and cracking abyss from which he will never wake up again.

Foreman Henkel climbs down to give the unconscious and dying man a final kick in the ribs with his heavy boots. Then he looks around. "Throw him behind the fence!" he whispers. "And any snitches can lie down right next to him, got it?"

That day, Mrs. Tennigkeit waited a long time for her son. It was to be in vain.

* * *

That same evening, as SA-Man Tennigkeit lies behind a construction fence in eternal slumber, his skull crushed and his guts torn apart, a National Socialist assembly in the Berlin center is crashed.

Just as their need is greatest, they barely manage to alarm the SA in time. The SA is currently enjoying a visit by Dr. Goebbels reminiscing about the fighting in the Ruhr area.

"You must attack again and again," he says, "again and yet again..."

The telephone rattles into his story.

The Doctor immediately reaches for the phone. "Attack?... The Commune?... Yes, we're coming!"

"We're coming!!!" the SA yells.

There is no hesitation. They hail five taxis and head for the city center.

There they break into the hall, with the Doctor, who could be done in by a single Red Front blow, right at the head.

In just under a quarter of an hour the hall is cleared of any and all Commune members.

Karl and Kurt laugh at each other with bright red cheeks.

"Well, what do you think of the Doctor?"

No answer is necessary.

4

LIMITS

The worker Schulz has taken to the streets once again, but his mood is no longer resigned. He is filled with an almost painful restlessness. He is freezing inside and out. Four weeks in prison for assault and battery—not exactly a relaxed vacation.

All this time he was asking himself, pondering whether the real reason for his imprisonment were those slaps or that cursed NSDAP. He reaches no conclusion. All he knows for sure is that the rubber truncheon was meant for the NSDAP. He isn't even sure why he claimed to be a Nazi. He feels unsure about anything and everything lately—the world and he do not quite agree with each other.

Dejected, he trots around the corner of Belle Alliance and Bergmannstraße. *Actually,* he thinks, *I ought to go to these Nazis and tell them: I did time for you, I took a beating for you, so now I belong to you, right?*

Then he thinks of Grey Eyes. Lately he's thinking about him a lot. Was that a worker? Are there any workers with the Nazis? He needs to figure out what that was all about.

He stops absent-mindedly in front of an advertising pillar at Zossener Eck. A blood-red poster has been put up there. *The Commune,* he thinks, when suddenly he realizes that this poster is not at all about the Commune.

"Come to the mass meeting!" it says. "Spandau," it continues in big letters. "Gauleiter Dr. Joseph Goebbels speaks on the subject: The German Worker and Socialism... Open debate for SPD and KPD... German workers, attend in droves!... NSDAP Berlin"

The worker Schulz examines this poster closely. First, this Goebbels has courage, and that's an extremely important topic: The German Worker and Socialism.

Schulz, listen, are you a German worker or not? Yes? Well, then let's go, Schulz, off to Spandau!

And Schulz counts his pennies. Fifty pennies.

OK, Schulz, for fifty pennies you can get to Spandau.

But before Schulz gets there, he is about to experience something that will drive a cold chill through his bones.

He stops at Bergmannstraße. A small funeral procession is making its way down the street. It is a pitiful sight: a tiny coffin, pulled by two emaciated nags. There are perhaps a hundred people trudging behind the carriage, and they fit in perfectly with the whole procession—as poor as the coffin, as starved as the horses.

The men are wearing old, patched military coats or worn out overcoats with sleeves that have grown far too short; the women are in shawls and shabby felt hats.

Silently and modestly they walk next to each other. They look neither to the right nor the left. Some men carry hats in their hands and stare about aimlessly.

At Marheinekeplatz they are coming to a sudden halt. A puzzled Schulz sees the coachman pulling his horses back. Then a stone comes flying.

Why are they throwing stones? he thinks in amazement and indignation. But then he has to make a quick retreat into an entrance, because now the funeral procession is getting pelted in stones.

Young boys and broads run around the hearse, cussing and chasing women, children, and men apart. *Have they gone mad?* Schulz thinks, unable to comprehend the ghastly sight.

Now he sees that the poor horses are bleeding; they climb up, frightened, and now they bolt. Volleys of stones are hurled after them, countless stones. The carriage swings back and forth and the little coffin with it, until just ahead of Schleiermacherstraße it slides off the carriage and crashes onto the pavement.

The worker Schulz turns pale, so absorbed is he by this completely incomprehensible turn of events. He stares at the coffin that is now lying in the middle of the street, cracked and torn open.

The two horses race on towards Hasenheide, while the women in their shabby shawls and felt hats just stand about the entrances, crying loudly and with a violent tremble in their limbs. Some have fallen to the ground unconscious; others have fixed their gazes on a man lying unmoving in the street, his tattered, grey military coat about him.

In front of the market hall the traders cackle excitedly, and over this curious cackling Schulz now hears cries of "Red Front! Red Front! Red Front!"

Sirens can be heard, and when the riot squad turns the corner, the street is already quiet and empty. Policemen recapture the horses, lift the small, poor coffin back onto the cart, gather the frightened men and women back together, help the beaten down man back on his feet and lead him away. Then the police car slowly follows the funeral procession.

Schulz shakes his head. What kind of hateful man are they trying to bury here?

Then he finds out the shocking truth. The person in the coffin was but a child. The dead child of Germans who had been expelled from the Soviet state of Russia. The dead child of people who were a little uncomfortable to the Bolsheviks.

Reason enough for the "Red Front!" and its bricks.

The worker Schulz remains motionless for a long time, staring behind the disappearing funeral procession in the distance. He does not realize how pale he has become, filled with shame and anger. He looks around to see a young boy standing next to him in a Russian tunic with a Soviet star fastened to it. For a moment, he stares at the pale, wet, pimpled face.

Then he punches the guy right in the face. The boy doesn't say much; he wipes his mouth, holds his cheeks, and absently stares at Schulz. The bystanders don't say much either; only one woman, standing behind the group gathered at her front door with two small children, remarks loud and clear, "He had that coming for a while now."

But the worker Schulz just gets on a street car and drives to Spandau.

* * *

The hall in Spandau is hung with thick clouds of smoke. Murmurs, talk, chatter, and gossip fill the assembly. From time to time exclamations can be heard from a corner; sometimes people shout incomprehensible sentences for the whole room to hear. The air is thick in every sense of the word.

On the tables the worker Schulz can see heaps of beer glasses, this classic ammunition of all political mass gatherings. He also sees that there are lots of Red Front men scattered all over the room, estimating their number at about five hundred. His estimate is not far off.

The Red Front men seem to be in excellent spirits; their gathering is almost picturesque. They toast each other, raise their hands, clench them into fists. They wave those fists back and forth. To Schulz, it almost looks as if they were taking measurements to prepare for their first blows.

Silently, he wonders at the naivety of Dr. Goebbels, who really seems to assume that these five hundred men did come with honest intentions to have a decent and objective discussion. They seem much more willing to give the Rhenish Doctor a thorough proletarian thrashing, without much idle chatter. Caught up in these considerations, the worker Schulz forces his way towards the platform. It is not the first political meeting he has attended, and he has developed a certain sixth sense, a premonition of the things to come.

For instance, he is absolutely certain that tonight there will be a brawl in this very hall. Awakening the old field soldier within him, he almost automatically decides on a Red Front man whose ugly mug he is eager to flatten out once the time is right.

You can hardly blame him for this crude intention; you can't justify or wax poetically about it either. Ever since he saw that child's coffin, the worker Schulz simply feels a dull ache raging at the back of his head, and that's all.

He looks around to discover an SA-Man near him. Schulz says, "Evening."

The SA-Man looks attentively at the man greeting him. One has to be suspicious even of a harmless greeting, if one doesn't want to be taken by surprise and ridiculed tonight.

"Heil Hitler!" says the SA-Man.

"Thick air in here, huh?" Schulz confides.

But the SA-Man only answers, "Maybe." Then he remains silent.

And then suddenly a huge noise breaks out in the hall, shouts of "Red Front!" and "Heil Hitler!" are mixed up. Schulz climbs on a chair, and at first he sees nothing but a forest of raised hands.

Then, at the back of the hall, he discovers a group of tall SA-Men next to the entrance, who are moving towards the platform in close formation. Schulz cannot quite see what is going on.

But then the group comes closer, and now Schulz discovers a small, pale man coming forward, his head raised high and flanked by strong men in brown shirts. To the left and right he greets with his outstretched hand, and with each smile his snow-white teeth light up again and again.

Schulz grumbles contentedly; he likes this smile. In fact, he likes that entire face very much.

Within that seemingly never-ending hurricane, the Doctor climbs onto the platform. Then things grow reasonably quiet, and immediately his first terse sentences rush into the hall.

"The National Socialist German Workers' Party debates openly with every honest people's comrade! Each party will be given sufficient time to speak. But first, I want to make it very clear for all of the attendants: this is our gathering. We determine the agenda, and if anyone disobeys this agenda, we will ruthlessly expel him or her to the fresh air!"

For a while, there is complete silence. SA faces remain motionless; the Red Front men are flabbergasted. Schulz, who was tremendously pleased with this opening, feels as if the five hundred were gasping for air, like fish on dry land. Schulz enthusiastically rubs his beer glass with both hands. He likes that man up there immensely, immensely!

Then Dr. Goebbels begins his speech. And although he generally doesn't care for more stylized speech, Schulz likes what he hears. This speech is amazingly descriptive, but also forceful, a tremendous, yet hidden force and an immense, entirely apparent hatred.

He talks about the socialism that was promised to the German worker for a generation. Again and again he quotes their empty phrases—they're all that's left of this promised socialism.

Schulz has to admit, this man does not mince his words.

At first there is a hail of random interjections, but then they slowly abate, becoming more modest and quieter. And finally the miracle happens. He is able to finish his speech in complete silence.

Schulz has never experienced something like this. *Well,* he thinks, *let's hear what the other speakers have to say.*

He sees one of these other gentlemen climbing onto the platform, about to start his speech, when suddenly things at the back of the hall are becoming restless. It turns out that two SA-Men have been attacked and beaten down in the street outside.

Almost immediately, Dr. Goebbels appears on the podium, brusquely cutting off the astonished communist speaker. On the podium stands the Gauleiter of Berlin.

"It is beneath the NSDAP's dignity," his cutting voice announces, "to continue allowing the speeches of a cowardly party's representatives. A cowardly party, whose followers try to make up for their lack of arguments by nightly ambushes with club and dagger. We are unwilling to endure this kind of abuse for even another second."

A hail of applause from the party comrades almost blows the hall to pieces. And not even Schulz could guess what is about to happen next. In fact, he would have deemed it impossible.

The communist speaker gets handed from one SA-Man to the next, until the entire SA seems to have become a single assembly line, and on this assembly line the Red Front men slip, stumble, fall, and whiz towards the fresh air.

The worker Schulz did not even get the chance to deal with his chosen Red Front mug. He is extremely pleased by this turn of events and trots contentedly towards the exit.

But as he makes his way there, he is restrained by a bright voice. He turns around to see a man standing on a chair, and God knows, this man is quite familiar to him. It is Grey Eyes.

Grey Eyes roars, "Join the SA! SA recruiting over here!"

And the worker Schulz slowly returns, greeting Grey Eyes on his chair, "Good evening. Remember me? I need one of those forms."

Schulz walks up to an empty table, sits down, pushes the beer glasses aside, and carefully fills in the registration form for the SA of the National Socialist German Workers' Party.

5

RESISTANCE

The next evening SA-Man Schulz reads *Die Rote Fahne.*[9] It is not his first time reading this newspaper, but today he reads it with particular curiosity.

Die Rote Fahne is boiling mad. According to them, the Spandau meeting was nothing but a single, brutal attack on the harmless and defenceless workers of Spandau.

Bold headlines above the description announce, "Nazis organize bloodbath in Spandau!" and "Sounding the alarms for the entire revolutionary workforce of the Reich capital!"

SA-Man Schulz grins. Nothing actually happened, but it makes him wonder what these dogs are going to write if finally something does happen. He rereads the closing sentence of the editorial, "This will cost you dearly!"

Then he puts the paper in his pocket. *Cost us dearly! We'll wait and see,* he thinks, and the word "we" fills him with joy. Finally he is no longer alone in the world. Now he belongs to something. It has become clear to him that he is rising, rising against the slow decline of his fatherland, rising together with all the other men of the swastika. And God willing, one day there will be enough of them to be able to help the fatherland rise once more.

Another day Schulz is present when Dr. Goebbels commissions a new poster, which only twenty-four hours later is glued to all the advertising pillars in Berlin, a huge, blood-red poster.

---

[9] *Die Rote Fahne (The Red Flag)* was a socialist newspaper, originally founded in 1876 by Socialist Party leader Wilhelm Hasselmann. During the time of the Weimar Republic, it was used as a publishing organ by Karl Liebknecht, Rosa Luxemburg, and their Spartacus League. After their death, it continued to reflect Communist Party opinion.

The bourgeois state is coming to an end! And rightly so!
For it is no longer able to free Germany!
A new Germany must be forged, a Germany that is no longer a
state of citizens and classes, a Germany of work and discipline!

History has chosen you for this task:
Workers of the brow and the fist!
The fate of the German people is in your hands!
Remember that! Stand up and act!

On Friday, 11th of February, 8PM,
Dr. Goebbels will speak in the Pharus Halls,
North Berlin, Müllerstraße 124, on:
The collapse of the bourgeois class state!

So the poster reads, and the Commune roars in insane fury. This was the greatest provocation ever put in front of them. *Die Rote Fahne* shouts itself hoarse:

"Whoever dares to tread the soil of North Berlin ought to know that he will get acquainted with the hard fists of the Berlin proletariat! Not a single fascist will leave the Pharus Halls alive! Beat them to a pulp, the labor-murderers who dare to even enter the halls which host the revolutionary proletariat's gatherings! At the place where Karl and Rosa[10] spoke to the proletariat, where leaders of the world revolution issued their stirring proclamations of revolutionary mass struggle, where not even the social fascists of the SPD dare to speak, here this utter rogue, this bandit of Berlin should be allowed to speak his provocations?

Proletariat of Berlin!

Defend yourself against the bloody fascist hordes!

You gentlemen of the swastika, remember it:

On Friday the revolutionary proletariat will be there!

On Friday, workers' fists will break you!

Red Wedding[11] belongs to the red proletariat!

Long live Soviet Russia! Long live the world revolution!"

---

[10] Karl Liebknecht and Rosa Luxemburg, prominent Jewish Communist intellectuals and politicians who played important roles during the November Revolution of 1918–1919 until they were executed by Freikorps troops.

[11] Wedding was a working-class district in North Berlin, the KPD's stronghold in the Reich Capital.

This was the Commune's response to Dr. Goebbels' poster. It sounded damned serious. The NSDAP and its Berlin Gauleiter had bet the Reich capital movement's fate on a single card.

And this time, even indifferent circles started to notice. The whole of Berlin got nervous. Whole districts in the north and east became feverish. Masses of politically experienced workers were well aware that an enormous brawl was inevitable.

Naturally the bourgeois and social-democratic newspapers were issuing anxious demands for a ban on this assembly. Meanwhile the SA takes to its listening posts. Their patrols wear civilian clothes and flood the area around the Pharus Halls in pairs.

Grey Eyes takes the new SA-Man Schulz with him, and on this occasion Schulz finally learns his new friend's full name.

"My name is Karl Schindler by the way," says Grey Eyes, "I'm a working student, do you mind?"

Schulz grumbles something, expressing his total indifference to that fact. And then they march off together.

The gathering is supposed to take place that same evening, so the battlefield has to be explored and studied.

"It can't be that bad," says Schulz, "they can't do more than beat us to death."

Karl gives him a sideways look. Then he remarks seriously, "Yes, they can. They can do way more than beat you to death. Don't know that yet, do you? There are worse things. And if they get the chance, they will. You should have been there at Leuna [12] and in Upper Silesia. [13] They weren't human anymore, I can tell you that much..."

Karl breaks off, he doesn't like to talk about it. To him it will forever remain a gruesome mystery how it could have been possible for brothers of the same homeland, brothers of the same people, brothers of the same blood to behave against each other like cruel beasts.

Schulz interrupts his musings. "Oh, I get it!" says the old field soldier Schulz. "Stuff like that? We had that in Belgium too, nothing to be done about it. It's the beast inside of men."

---

[12] A town in Saxony-Anhalt, primarily known for its chemical industry. In 1923 it was the center of an armed communist uprising in middle Germany, known as the March Action. The uprising was eventually quelled by government troops.

[13] After the end of the First World War, Upper Silesia remained a part of the German Reich. A plebiscite was planned to give the local population the choice to stay part of the Reich or defect to Poland and Czechoslovakia. During the years prior to the plebiscite in 1922, a number of armed uprisings took place.

Karl gives his comrade another secret sideways look. Karl is twenty years old and has only experienced the war back home. He always had tremendous respect for the men who have been in the field. Suddenly, Grey Eyes grows a little shy. "Really?" he says. "So you had to deal with those beasts as well..."

SA-Man Schulz nods. "Not just once. But you know what I feel like today? Man, it's just like it was back at Kemmel.[14] Lying in a dugout, you hear nothing, see nothing, and you're shivering from top to bottom. Not out of fear; you just shiver, you know? And you've got such a rage inside of you. You get showered in artillery fire left and right, and the attack is in four hours—four hours until it's go time. Then you have to get out of your hole. Whether you'll come back, no one knows. But you don't care either way. Maybe you come back, maybe you don't. But everyone knows they're getting out. And you know why they go out instead of staying inside their holes?"

Karl remains silent.

Sergeant Schulz carries on with his explanation, "Because you know what's going on. Because that's the way it has to be. Because you know that there is a meaning behind it. Because it's one for all and all for one. And that is just what I feel like today."

Alert and vigilant, they patrol the entire neighborhood of the Pharus Halls. They pass by other SA-Men whom they do not officially know, and they both know exactly what they need to pay attention to.

"Three piles of stones to the left," Karl says, secretly noting down this ammunition depot.

"Flowerless flower pots in the corner house," Schulz reports and Karl notes this down as well.

"Pub to the left," says Schindler, "narrow entrance next to it. Remember that small pub. It's called Altes Feldschlösschen, written above the door. If you have to take off, don't go in there. They don't like us in there."

In front of Altes Feldschlösschen lurks a young, fat guy with a cold cigarette stuck to his lower lip. Every now and then he swings at the hips a little and adjusts his peaked blue cap, his long black hair almost falling on his nose. Now he gives a fleeting glance to the two SA-Men before he turns around to say a few quiet words to the open door. Then he turns around again, towards the street.

---

[14] Kemmel is the name of both a village and a hill formation in Belgium. In the First World War, it was the site of ferocious battles between French and German troops.

"Watch out!" Karl whispers.

The young lad slowly starts to move and strolls over to them. Sluggish and treacherous pupils are hiding behind his heavy eyelids. "Never been to this area, eh?" he says, barely moving his lazy lips.

But Karl knows exactly what to make of this apparent laziness, and so does the worker Schulz. He knows this type well enough.

"Won't be a stranger for much longer," says Schulz, "got a girl here. You know a place to stay?"

"Nah. What about him?" The guy points his fat chin at Karl, hands hidden inside his pockets.

"He helps me search."

They get another lazy look; then the guy stays behind, turning his head to watch them every now and then. Now he joins a group standing in front of the Altes Feldschlösschen. That very moment Schulz and Karl turn right into the next building entrance and gleefully race through three courtyards before they leisurely re-emerge on Brüsseler Straße.

"There we go," says Schulz, visibly satisfied.

It's only four o'clock in the afternoon, but the streets in this area are already full of people. Most of them are still idling around, gathering in front of shop windows, standing next to building entrances, or strolling up and down. A strange heat is steaming in these streets, a heat that isn't caused by sun or air.

At five o'clock the crowds slowly but steadily start to approach the Pharus Halls. At half past five, the building hums like an immense beehive. People squeeze themselves into the entrances incessantly.

At six o'clock the Pharus Halls are full.

At seven o'clock they are closed down by the police.

Schulz and Schindler have positioned themselves near the podium. They stubbornly remain near a corner table, knowing full well about its tactical advantages. On that table, they have wordlessly amassed a dozen beer glasses.

With every minute, the hall feels more like a greenhouse. One can hardly move without breaking a sweat. It is impossible to see the whole length of the room, its far corners completely obscured by clouds of blue smoke.

Schulz and Schindler calmly watch the turmoil. Without much calculation, they realize that two thirds of all participants belong to the Commune. They are not particularly worried about it.

The Commune drinks. Heaps of empty beer glasses form on all

tables. The Commune drinks not because of their unquenchable thirst; they simply want to get more empty beer glasses. And the two SA-Men notice this as well.

Every now and then a shrill female voice can be heard screaming. Sometimes a rumble goes along the walls. The crater of people at the center of the room emits a constant jumble of voices. Like the surf of a sea, noises surge up and down, becoming quieter and then louder again.

By now, the Pharus Halls are nothing more than an overheating cauldron of human bodies, and each human body in return is nothing but an overheating vessel of passions.

At this moment, as Schulz recognizes all of this with just a few glances, he feels proud, as never before in those days. The pride of being an SA-Man. He looks around for his comrades.

The SA remains cold and indomitable.

The faces of these men are motionless. And this steadfastness is not a military pose, but an expression of their terrible seriousness. They know the disastrous jungle they have ventured into and are determined not to be misled. None of them can be sure whether he will not wake up in a hospital that evening—or maybe not at all.

But they do not worry about that. They have to protect their Gauleiter, the Doctor who is foolhardy enough to grab this most mischievous, cruel, and vile enemy of theirs by the neck.

The SA remains cold and indomitable.

Around eight o'clock a very inelegant, decrepit car rumbles along Müllerstraße. It has to drive very slowly near the Pharus Halls, because the road is filled by thick crowds of people.

A quiet rain sets in. In front of the halls stands a human wall, and a never-ending chant thunders forth from it:

"Red Front–

Beats the fascists–

To pulp, to pulp, to pulp."

Like an eerie choir, this battle cry echoes from the walls of nearby houses.

The Doctor's face in the car is narrow, his skin lying strangely taut over his cheekbones, his lips slightly curled in a mocking smile. Two dark eyes burn towards the SA leader, who is now laboriously paving a way through the dense crowd.

"Pharus Halls have been closed down by the police since an hour ago!" he reports. "Two thirds Red Front. Trouble's brewing!"

Goebbels thanks him.

As he enters the hall, it feels like the ceiling is collapsing amidst bursting walls; so hellish is his welcome. Just as the Doctor takes his first steps towards the podium, a guy wants to pounce on him, but is restrained by the powerful fists of a Red Front leader.

"Gently, my boy, gently," grins the Red Front man as he pushes the boy behind him, "let him arrive first. We want to get a good look at this clown before we start pulling his leg."

The Doctor gives the man a cold look and continues his walk. From his perspective it must seem as if the entire three thousand people present were Red Front. Crowds of people rage towards him. Distorted grimaces left and right, hate, hate, hate.

"Rent boy!"

"Labor-killer!"

"Bloodhound!"

"Fascist pig!"

"Dirty bastard!"

"Just come and get some!"

"Crush that dog!"

"Down, down, down!"

"Hail Moscow! Hail Moscow!"

"Smash his face already!"

"God damn lout!"

Like all of his comrades, the SA-Man Schulz remains cold and indomitable amidst this erupting volcano of rage and hate. Right now, his thoughts are strange, almost gentle. He wonders what being exposed to these torrents of filth must feel like to a human being. To a simple man, he thinks, it may not even matter, but to this little Doctor, a man of quality and education, a man of feeling and imagination, scientifically trained and with a carefully honed brain, someone who looks as if he might not be quite up to these rough, ruthless challengers...

Suddenly, another whirlwind of voices tears Schulz away from his tender worries.

The SA is no longer cold and indomitable.

A raging, sky-high fountain shoots forth from the SA, hurling everything else aside, a tornado arising from every nook and cranny:

"Heil Hitler!"

"Heil Hitler!"

"Heil Hitler!"

Torrents of screeches and roars crash against this call in a vain attempt to try and wash it away. Sometimes it seems as if they were to succeed, but again and again Schulz hears the calls of the SA and the party roaring through the storm, while he himself is screaming his lungs off.

The hall increasingly resembles a raving lunatic asylum, and within this madhouse, the meeting's SA leader, Daluege[15] by name, tries to calm things down to open the meeting.

It is impossible.

When he raises his hand, a thousand voices roar scorn and laughter towards him. The Doctor peers almost thoughtfully into this bursting human scenery.

Suddenly, the faces of Karl and Schulz appear gaunt. These are the faces of men who are headed for the storm, leaving behind any emotion that could still distract them. Right now, there are no more feelings.

A very tall SA-Man walks by them, giving them a cold look.

"It's about to start!" he mutters hoarsely, his eyes sparkling. He nods as if to cheer them up, then climbs onto the podium.

The louder it gets in the hall, the quieter they speak on the podium, and the more attentively they observe the room.

The tall SA-Man has stepped behind the Doctor, whispering into his ear, "Doctor, if this goes wrong, we're done for."

"And if it goes well," the Doctor replies almost cheerfully, "then we've done it for good."

Down in the hall, the Commune is changing tactics. It hasn't exactly become quieter, but their voices have become more uniform and not quite as provocative. One can understand some individual calls.

And now their tactics are becoming apparent: As soon as the chairman begins to speak, a guy somewhere in the hall stands up and shouts, "To the agenda!"

And a thousand Red Front men join in the shout, "To the agenda!"

Schulz abruptly turns around on his heel as if stung by an adder—he heard someone close to him screaming this stupid interjection. Focusing on the perpetrator, he gives Karl a nudge. "Hey, I know that

---

[15] Kurt Daluege, an early SA leader in Berlin who later went on to join the SS and lead the German police force. After being extradited to Czechoslovakia, he was executed in Prague in 1946.

guy!"

"Feldschlösschen!" replies Karl. And suddenly Schulz remembers. Of course! It was that fat mealworm who had approached them. He squeezes his eyes shut and commits the boy to memory.

And then Schulz and Karl no longer dare to turn their eyes away from the podium. Something seems to be going on. The little Doctor and his companions have taken on a menacing aspect. They now stand completely motionless, silently staring down into the hall as if they were searching for something. And then something incomprehensible happens. Schulz has to bite his lips in order to stay quiet. Dr. Goebbels suddenly bends forwards, while the SA-leader slightly raises one of his hands.

Schulz can see a group of uniformed SA-Men, bold, silent and upright, cold and serious, marching directly into the midst of hell, into this roaring, wheezing, howling hell. With an almost mechanistic precision, they work their way through the raging crowd and sweep one of the main screamers off his chair. They drag him through the hall, and before anyone even understands what is going on, the screamer stands on the podium, completely pale and trembling. And in that very heartbeat, Schulz and Karl know what is about to happen.

And it happens. After a brief moment of astonished silence, the Commune explodes.

Karl yells, "Heads down!" and at the same moment the first beer glass shatters on the wall behind them. Just barely, they can see the arrested screamer throwing himself off the podium back into the crowd and then...

Then the real battle begins.

The hall has transformed into an inferno. Three thousand people beating and roaring. Beer glasses flash through the smoke and end up shattering everywhere, on tables, walls, faces. Bursts of shards pour down like hail. With an insane howling, people break chairs, chair legs are being swung, and already one can hear the first screams of the injured.

In the middle of the hall a group of Red Front men has formed. Standing in close formation on chairs and tables, they sweep huge volleys of beer glasses towards the podium. The SA and the little Doctor are battered by a torrent of sharp, glass splinters.

Lamps shatter, bottles have been brought in and whirl over the assembled heads, plates cut through the air, more glasses burst, and people are going down, writhing on the floor. Sobbing, they try to escape from being trampled.

The battle has become insane.

The incessant roaring, screaming, shouting, sobbing, crying and wailing, moaning, cursing, and panting have turned into a collective, concentrated scream in which one can no longer distinguish between individual sounds.

The Commune has become a raging beast, and the cause of Adolf Hitler seems lost. Their attack has begun with such force and is being carried on with such exceptional bitterness that it seems like the National Socialists have simply been swept away.

But if there can be such a thing as the sacred will of the Führer, then now this holy will of their distant leader seizes the SA and every party comrade in the room.

Almost as if there had been an inaudible command, the unfurling of an invisible banner, or the arrival of a sudden signal, an unprecedented turn of events is taking place.

The Nazis have risen to attack.

Their arms work furiously; their fists are drumming. Their hands are empty, no chair legs, beer glasses, knives, or bottles. They clean up with their naked fists. And they're not exactly dealing with straw dolls here. Blood runs down their faces. Many of them collapse, buried under bottles and beer glasses. Entire chairs are broken over their heads. But every SA-Man on the floor who is still conscious rolls around with a Red Front man and does not let go of him.

The SA works like a carefully selected, precisely trained, magnificent Storm Troop.

Schulz and Schindler have long since climbed onto the grandstand, and from up here they hurl down one beer glass after another. To his great delight, Schulz comes across a few dozen bottles. Now he is no longer SA-Man Schulz, but non-commissioned officer Schulz, third company, hand grenade specialist. Bottle after bottle whirls from his well-trained hands. So gripped is he by the curious rapture of battle that Karl next to him starts to wonder about his completely incomprehensible shouts accompanying each throw:

"Twenty-one!"

"Twenty-two!"

"Twenty-three!"

And then the bottle sweeps through the hall in a flat curve. Karl does not know that this is the firing formula for sharp hand grenades—he had been a child during the war. At "twenty-three" the grenade must be out of your hands if you don't want it blowing up in your own face.

Puddles of blood, bundles of people, shattered tables. The first communists flee from the hall. Some of the wounded manage to drag themselves out. In front of the Pharus Halls a huge crowd steams and trembles with excitement. They hear the rampage and shouting, hear the splintering and crashing; they can see bleeding communists leaving the halls. And now all hell is breaking loose under the open sky as well.

It sounds like a hundred thousand women howling and screaming in unison.

After maybe fifteen minutes of murderous fighting, the SA knows that they have succeeded. More and more communists flee the room, and when an unconscious one wakes back up, he is faced by a room full of swastikas. Accordingly, he drags himself out as quickly as possible.

Now the other side of the battle becomes visible.

The hall is littered with rubble and debris. The stairs leading up to the grandstand, the podium, tables, a few surviving chairs, the floor itself, everything is red with blood. A terrible smell lies over the deserted battlefield. Paramedics are hurrying around.

Ten SA-Men must be taken away, badly injured.

And while the Commune continues to rage outside, the SA leader Daluege can be seen standing in his place on the podium. With an iron calm he announces, "The meeting continues! The speaker has the floor!"

Those present will never forget it: amidst blood and death, in a gruesome panorama of tattered chandeliers, tables and chairs, in the midst of a lake of shards and splinters, Dr. Joseph Goebbels begins to speak to the assembled National Socialists.

Paramedics and comrades remove the wounded. A telephone call for ambulances has been placed. They will arrive soon.

The police are nowhere to be seen.

Schulz has received a huge scrape, but it is not particularly serious. He worries about his friend Karl, whom he has suddenly lost sight of, but rediscovers him lying unconscious at the foot of the stairs. He can't quite make out what happened to him at first, so he puts Karl on his broad shoulders and carries him to an ambulance. As they leave the halls, Schulz receives his first shock of the night. Out here, things haven't calmed down, quite the opposite in fact. Communists are attacking the defenceless wounded, and the SA-Men coming outside are only barely able to save those poor guys from the brutal ordeal by carrying them back into the hall.

The commotion can be heard inside, and suddenly, they can also hear a cutting scream: "Dr. Goebbels!"

The Doctor interrupts his speech to rush outside, where a troubled SA is still guarding their injured from the inhuman horde. And here the Doctor bids farewell to his gravely injured comrades. He shakes hands with each of them, expressing his gratitude through warm and comforting words.

Then he returns to the hall and continues his speech.

Closing his oration, he speaks of those who are lying outside in their blood, and at that moment he utters those great and proud words for the unknown SA-Man,

"...who does his duty day after day, obeying a law he does not know and hardly understands. Who may get his skull smashed, simply because of his greatness, because he stands above the mob and leads the way for his people.

"But who nevertheless remains quiet, chaste, and brave in doing his duty for a kingdom that is about to come. Before him, we take off our caps and stand in reverence. One day, Germany will rise from his blood, the blood of the unknown warrior. Let us remember him!"

The assembly rises, silent, and deeply shaken.

Then the National Socialists march off through the raging and roaring Communist hordes, protected by the SA.

This evening was to decide the movement's fate in Berlin. The German freedom movement had begun its march in the Reich capital.

Over the next few days the wounded reappeared in their white bandages, wearing them like badges of honor. Often, the Doctor's eyes rest on them, and he knows exactly why.

Six hundred party members became three thousand.

6

Home

"Berlin stays red!" cries are everywhere. "Death to fascists!" announce the wall fronts. But the SA marches.

The SA fought the battle of the Pharus Halls, a handful of men.

"Berlin stays red!"

But Schulz and Karl are founding a Storm club.

In no time at all, Karl found them a cellar, a real, genuine top cellar. And the best thing about it is that it is only accessible from the street. The building entrance can be monitored by looking through a small hatch. This hatch is located right behind the front gate, so nobody gets in unless the SA lets him. The windows can be locked and also closed down from the inside with wooden shutters.

According to Schulz, they could also fit these shutters with sheet iron, so no bullet will get through. What's more, the walls are thick and solid, so they can make all the noise they want, and no one will be able to hear it either in the house or on the street outside.

"Well," says Schulz, "now what?"

"Do you know where we could find an old army cot?" Karl asks.

"No, why do you want one?"

"For the SA home of course!"

Schulz thinks about it. "No, I don't know of any cots, but I know where we could get plenty of boards. They are lying around near the Volkspark. And then we can make cots out of them. We need more than one anyway."

"And straw bags?"

"Well we can just stuff them ourselves."

"And the bed with straps underneath? So much nicer to sleep in."

"We'll need a table, too."

"Of course. And chairs, don't you think?"

"And maybe some sort of cabinet, right?"

"An oven, man, an oven! We'll want to be down there during winter as well!"

"It still is winter, man! So yes, an oven!"

"A few books would be nice too, don't you think? And a chess board and some cards!"

"And a few plates, right?"

"Some curtains for the windows wouldn't hurt either."

With curtains in mind, a luxurious idea, an image of comfort and cleanliness, Schulz insists on getting a door mat as well. "Don't want everyone to drag their dirt inside."

And then they get cocky and megalomaniacal.

"A coffee pot!"

"And a lamp of course!"

"And blankets for sleeping too!"

So they go to work. Schulz fetches the boards and Karl, Erich, Fritz, Ede, and Gerhard start tinkering and building. A worker, a coachman, a student, a waiter, a policeman, and an errand boy. Every evening they ruthlessly and relentlessly canvas their party comrades for anything that seems superfluous, anything that isn't bolted down. Getting two old quilts on one of those trips makes them giddy for a whole three days. The cellar's inauguration is a festive evening for the entire SA. It is the first SA club in Berlin. Their first place to stay! Their first home!

"Now we just need to worry about getting thrown out by the landlord," Schulz remarks, contentedly looking around their palace.

Karl flares up. "What? Then that landlord gets a proper thrashing by the party, he's not going to do any throwing after that."

They immediately agree on his plan of action.

There they sit, comfortable, cozy, together. Karl contributes an unbelievable amount of Wandervögel[16] songs, leading their coachman to teach them an equally unbelievable amount of solid, earthy Berlin songs, and then Schulz jokingly sings them a few communist songs. They are recomposed in no time at all, and with only a few changes they make for some rather bloodthirsty drinking songs.

Finally, Erich discovers his poetic side, and soon the first Storm songs make their debut in this smoky cellar, with harmonica, accordion and a few old guitars as a proper accompaniment.

---

[16] A German youth movement of the late nineteenth and early twentieth centuries, similar to the American Boy Scouts.

Die Rote Front, schlagt sie zu Brei,   *The Red Front, beat them to a pulp,*
S.A. marschiert, marschiert,   *SA marches and marches on,*
Die Straße frei!...   *Clear the road!...*

Brüder in Zechen und Gruben,   *Brothers in mines and pits,*
Brüder ihr hinter dem Pflug,   *You brothers behind the plough,*
Aus den Fabriken und Stuben   *Emerge from factories and barracks*
Folgt unseres Banners Zug!...   *To follow our banner's train!...*

Der mächtigste König im Luftrevier   *The mightiest king in the air*
Ist der sturmesgewaltige Aar,   *Is the storm-tossed eagle,*
Die Vögelein erzittern, vernehmen sie   *Smaller birds tremble, once they hear*
Sein rauschendes Flügelpaar!...   *His rustling span of wings!...*

Wir sind die Hitlergarde...   *We are the Hitler Guard...*

Draußen am Wiesenrand   *At the edge of the lawn,*
Hocken zwei Dohlen...   *Two jackdaws are sitting...*

The home grows and blossoms, becoming ever more homely. They actually managed to get some clean, smooth linoleum for their floor. The merchant next door donated it. They also set up a pot-bellied stove to make soup and coffee and maybe even roast a schnitzel if you happen to have one. Most of the time you don't.

Eventually, Schulz moves into the cellar for good. He worries that someone might damage or steal all their treasures. He also thinks that someone ought to be there to receive orders and answer questions, because little by little, they acquire certain things that need guarding—their small collection of rubber truncheons for example.

This collection is quite necessary, because unsurprisingly, the Commune already knows about the cellar. Already they can see unknown faces prowling around near the building.

The time has come when a brown shirt—worn in the street at night—can mean death. So it is getting more and more common that some of them have to stay in the cellar overnight.

It is Schulz who has a sixth sense for thick air outside. He watches over them like a mother, who can also be rough when necessary. "You're not leaving tonight!" he growls when his instincts kick in. "Here, have a book, or let's play some chess. Or we can sing. Let the Muscovites freeze their toes off. You're staying here."

He is the commander of this underground bunker. He secures the windows and locks the door; he watches the street from the hatch.

Then he withdraws to the stove and reads Eichendorff, whom he loves dearly ever since Karl first put a book of poetry in his hand. Or he hums his favorite song to himself: "Argonnerwald um Mitternacht."[17] That fits both together. Absolutely.

A large swastika flag emblazons their wall. He often finds himself silently staring at this flag, lost in that white field with the victorious swastika. Such power emanates from this symbol. One can feel it deep inside, just about where the soul should be.

Schulz once heard people talking about magic. He never understood much about that, nor did he think much of it. But in these nights, he understands everything.

One day, this banner must be flown in the world, or it will perish.

"Why?" someone asks him once.

"Dunno," Schulz shrugs his shoulders. "But that's how it is. All you have to do is look at it for a while. If you don't get it—well, then we can't use you."

Yes, that's the top cellar of the Third Reich—and the SA-Man Schulz—in the spring of 1927.

---

[17] "Argonnerwald um Mitternacht" ("Argonne Forest at Midnight") is a German pioneer song from the First World War. It would later be given new lyrics and adopted as a marching song by both the KPD and various NSDAP organizations, including the SA.

7

RECONNAISSANCE

It is an exciting spring.

The SA is already a power to be reckoned with. Every now and then, some of the Storms make their little visits to the Mark, ensuring people are aware that the Red Front has gotten competition—the SA.

In the Reich capital, SA-Men diligently stroll through the streets, observing the terrain on which they will have to fight again, sooner or later. They have been ordered to take care. So they stroll in plain clothes, without the brown shirt and trousers, without their SA cap.

Schulz takes great care that these wise instructions are observed in his area.

One day, a young lad visits the cellar with an SA cap on his head, fresh, cheerful, bold.

Schulz is amazed. "Have you gone completely mental?" he hisses. "It's enough if they bash in your head at a meeting, get it?" The boy looks at him somewhat dumbfounded, embarrassedly turning the cap in his hand.

Schulz turns a little milder. "You're proud of the cap, aren't you? You should be. You should be very proud! It's an honorable cap, just as honorable as a steel helmet. It just doesn't protect you as well. Don't look at me like that. If someone sees you with that cap at night, you'll get a brick in the neck and four knives through your ribs. That's the way it is in this fine town. But let me tell you something: I'd rather have a living SA-Man than one with an obituary. And so does the Führer. Everything in its time, you know?"

Hesitatingly, the boy asks, "So what am I supposed to do with the cap?"

Schulz rolls his eyes. "Well don't start chewing on it, idiot. Put it in your pocket. The cap won't mind. Be proud of carrying it in your pocket. And stop looking at me like a lost puppy. Caution is also the

40

mother of our SA service. Now come along, let's get going."

They go for a stroll.

It's one o'clock at night and the streets are filled with the intense aroma of spring, of March and warm winds. Girls walk slower than usual; they stop at the canal, gazing into the trees and the water until eventually their gaze loses itself somewhere in the distance and they start dreaming.

"Nice quarter," Schulz observes peacefully. "A bit too many houses, no panorama, but quite nice. When the balconies are in bloom, it'll look very neat. You see, as long as people are still watering their flower pots, they're not really communists at all... Now what's this?"

He has stopped near a wall where a poster of the Red Front Fighters' Federation has been put up. The clenched fist over the Soviet star invites passers-by to a unit gathering.

"Keep a lookout" Schulz grins, and the boy walks several feet away from him, looking in all directions. Schulz pulls out his cobbler knife and scrapes the poster from the wall with quick, broad cuts. The night wind playfully tears away the pieces, distributing them all over the street.

"There's another one over there," the boy reports.

"Well, keep another lookout," responds Schulz, and again the night winds do their part.

"And now," says Schulz, "let's go for a little sneak patrol in the enemy trench."

The boy is unsure what to make of this. They reach Hasenheide and indifferently pass by a number of amusement stalls. They stroll to Hermannplatz and turn into Boddinstraße.

At the third house to the left, Schulz discovers what he had hoped to see. There stands Karl Schindler, waiting. Schulz whistles, Karl whistles back, and then they stand together. Schulz nods at the boy. "Name's Hermann," he says.

The student shakes the boy's hand. Then he turns to Schulz. "No. 37 it is," he says softly.

Schulz nods satisfied. "Secret printing press," he explains to the boy, "by the Commune. Why they need a secret printing press, I have no clue. Not a clue in the world. After all, they are free to print all the crap they want at *Die Rote Fahne*, completely open. Let's have a look at the place. Everything clear, Karl?"

"Last one left around one o'clock. With a thick briefcase. But they may have left a guard inside."

"We'll know about that right away," says Schulz, "just a second, I've got a hairpin here somewhere. There it is."

Thirty seconds later, the front door swings open. Schulz seems to know what he's doing.

"Straight ahead," he whispers, "and then to the right. Don't even think about switching on that flash light, Hermann." They tiptoe through the hallway. On the right there is a staircase leading downwards. Schulz goes ahead.

"Everything fine?" whispers Karl.

"Fine."

They stop in front of a dark doorway. Schulz feels around for the safety lock, then searches for the celluloid strip in his breast pocket. A chain is carefully and expertly pressed out of its hinge.

A soft creak later, and the three of them find themselves in a hallway smelling of resin, alcohol, paint, oil, and turpentine. Karl sends a short flash of light through the hallway. At the end of it there is a heavy, iron-clad door.

"Watch out for traps," Schulz whispers. He knows their anti-intruder tricks. But everything goes well. This door has only a very simple lock and snaps open immediately. The SA has reached the communist secret printing works. Its windows are bolted, closed down with fixed shutters, and tightly hung with drapes.

Standing in front of a large wooden table, Karl whistles contentedly through his teeth. There it is—everything they were looking for. A jumble of photographs, right next to seals, passport forms, posters, lists, maps, and plans.

"There we go," says Schulz. He reaches for a notebook, quickly skimming through it.

"Murder list," he concludes and pockets the booklet.

Karl has calmly pulled up a chair to study the false passports and everything else. Extremely interesting stuff. There are Foreign Office seals as well as seals from four police precincts: Berlin, Essen, Hamburg, and Leipzig. There are seals from labor offices, rural worker accommodations, the Reichswehr Ministry as well as the Reichstag, Democratic Party seals, and now Karl even comes across an NSDAP seal. With a deep growl, he recovers the seal. Then he conscientiously selects ready-made passports, which are only lacking the photograph and gathers a few more seals for his collection. Finally, he delves into the plans that are lying about.

A curious Schulz watches over his shoulders. The old soldier immediately knows what these maps of Berlin, the Ruhr area, Hamburg, and Central Germany are supposed to mean. They are covered with red and blue circles, arrows, markings, crossroads, and barrier lines. "A proper general staff map," he appreciates, "plan of attack and all that."

Having chosen what they need, they take a closer look at the stove. The stove happens to be very practical for their purposes. In go the posters, shortly followed by the photographs. They break the photographic equipment, douse everything in alcohol and light the stove.

Meanwhile, Schulz discovers a small manual printing press lying in a corner. Sitting down at the table, a patient Schulz takes the time to painstakingly print a private poster:

HEIL HITLER!

They are finishing up their operation. Prominently placing the poster on the cleared table, they set off. Twenty minutes past three they return to their cellar to sort their loot.

Next morning, the Political Police headquarters at Alexanderplatz receive an anonymous tip. Boddinstraße. Secret printing press.

But the policemen are not in a hurry. And when they finally arrive at Boddinstraße, all they find is a wooden table with a poster on it, announcing in large print:

HEIL HITLER!

Otherwise, the capable officers find nothing and are left scratching their heads. What was that all about? Since when do communists print posters for Hitler?

Captain Fichtefachs at the police headquarters broods over this mysterious poster for a full hour. He has lost some faith in this world.

8

AMBUSH

It is a beautiful March Sunday and Storm 1 marches to Trebbin for the first annual Mark Day.[18] Everyone who has time tags along, and those who don't, come along anyway.

"We'll show those lads what we're about!"

But Storm 1 doesn't just want to parade through the Mark, they also want to get a breath of fresh air while they're at it. To roam around the woods again, watching tender birch trees turn green, fields of corn growing towards the light, the view of white clouds above wide meadows and murmuring streams. The Berlin SA had to go without this for a long time. They are at the front lines of a gigantic asphalt battlefield and have neither time nor patience for poetic musings. They have been ordered to bring about the Third Reich. This sobering, manly task is hard and brutal, exposing them to blood and danger at every waking hour.

The SA enjoys its march into the Mark.

Flags are waving in Trebbin, both the black-white-red and the swastika variety. Farmers and farm laborers have gathered from all over, these earthy men who never caught on to the hysterical idea that their fatherland could be the whole world and that a fatherland could be anywhere. Now they stand in the streets and are somewhat incredulously watching the brown columns marching along in lock step.

Amidst roars, cracking and rustling, the brown columns parade towards Daluege and Goebbels.

Flowers come flying, and the brown shirts are left to wonder where all of those flowers came from in early March. The people of the Mark

---

[18] Mark Brandenburg, the rural areas surrounding Berlin. Trebbin is a town in Brandenburg, which in the 1930s was home to roughly 3500 inhabitants.

have plundered the nurseries to get flowers. Early flowers from Markish greenhouses decorate the SA-Men.

Smiling girls stand by the wayside; since time immemorial girls have watched and smiled whenever something marched along in lock step.

And these here are soldiers, soldiers of the Third Reich, which the German lands are dreaming about, guardsmen of Adolf Hitler.

Songs are resonating throughout the Mark.

Swastika on steel helmet
Black-white-red band
Sturmabteilung Hitler
We are called.

Farmers wave their hats; girls and women are waving as well. Boys with bright red cheeks run up and down the length of the parade like greyhounds.

The day passes by like a dream: in the Mark Brandenburg countryside, under white clouds, amidst countless songs.

In the evening, parts of the SA drive back towards Berlin on trucks. The others are to be transported to Lichterfelde [19] in special Reichsbahn[20] wagons. In Lichterfelde, they want to meet up again for their march back to Berlin.

Waving, goodbyes, calls from all sides, jokes and laughter.

"Heil Hitler!"

"Heil Hitler!"

For those who travel by train, two carriages have been reserved in the scheduled train.

It has become impossible to tell whether it was a coincidence or criminal negligence by the dispatcher, but for some reason the very same train the SA now boarded had already been occupied by several hundred Red Front fighters. A more explosive combination would be difficult to imagine. As for distribution, the usual Sunday audience occupied the front car, SA the second car, Red Front men in the third and then again SA in the fourth.

The outcome was inevitable.

---

[19] An area in the South-West of Berlin.

[20] The *Reichsbahn* was the German national railway system in service between 1920 and 1949.

At first there were shouts.

The SA does not care. They had a wonderful day behind them and are not going to let the Red Front spoil their good mood. Besides, they want to preserve their strength for the march on Berlin later today. That really is more important than some stupid insults or a useless brawl.

But the red front shouts do not let up, and unsurprisingly the SA gradually gets angrier. But their squad leaders remain strict. Their voices are sharp, "Do not reply! Do not provoke! No clashes! We leave this train calm and disciplined! We pass by the communist car right away and head for the exit!"

Slowly the train enters the Lichterfelde-East station. Just like they have been ordered, the SA-Men quickly jump out of their wagons and hurry towards the exit. They look neither left nor right; they do not honor the shouts and insults with a single word. In this fateful moment, a shot is fired. An SA-Man throws up his arms before he collapses silently. For a moment the entire platform freezes in horror.

And then all hell breaks loose.

Squad leader Geyer races towards the stationmaster, who has police authority on the platform, asking him to identify the shooter, but before he reaches the officer, a bullet hits him. It hits exactly on his belt buckle where the metal sheet slightly reduces its impact.

The good squad leader Geyer staggers, trying to take a few more steps; then he collapses. Shot after shot whips out of the train. The platform reverberates hundreds of times, horribly distorting the sound of the shots, almost like an infantry battle. Again and again the sounds of pistol shots rattle the air.

The SA behaves like a veteran troop. They take cover and jump off the platform, onto the tracks. Now the train slowly starts to move again. The SA has taken cover because there was no point in exposing themselves to open fire on the platform. But they have no intention of letting murderers escape. At the last moment an SA-Man jumps onto the moving train, climbs into the next compartment and pulls the emergency brake. With a horrible screeching, the wheels come to a halt.

The train stops.

The communists fire like there's no tomorrow. Maybe they can guess what is coming next. SA-Man Teichert sinks to the ground, his blood running over the stone slabs.

Meanwhile the trucks from Trebbin have arrived at the station; it is the Spandau SA section. They are accompanied by Dr. Goebbels and many civilian party comrades who want to join the march. At first they cannot comprehend what is going on. They hear the whipping sound of shots and the screams of the wounded. And then they begin to understand.

No command is needed. No agreement is necessary. None of them stop to think for even a single second. They jump off their trucks, columns break formation, and everyone storms forwards, through the tunnel, up the stairs.

But the railway officials have closed the doors and hastily locked everything.

No one can get through.

With feverish foreheads, twitching fists, and flaming rage, the Spandau SA is forced to leave the comrades to their fates.

But the fifty men up on the platform are no longer hesitating. They tear apart their flagpoles whose tips are still lined with wartime bayonets, a French and a Russian one. They also have stones from the railway embankment. And then they have their fists, combined with a colossal anger at the cowardly ambush.

With these weapons the SA attacks, trying to get the Reds out of their wagons. They try it a second and a third time. Success does not come easy to them. The Reds duck down and hold the doors closed from the inside. In the first wagon, rapidly deserted by the Sunday crowd, the SA-Men find a Jewish-looking man. He lies flat on the floor, only coming up for quick looks out the window every now and then.

Bitter and suspicious, the SA people pull him to his feet. They punch his face until the horrified man exclaims a few foreign words. One of the SA-Men understands them to be Spanish and stops his comrades. A foreigner!

Then they finally manage to bypass the train so they can attack from two sides. Still there are gunshots coming from the train. The SA stalks closer. This much they know: nobody will escape. Even if they have to stay here all night, this train won't leave until the last of these cowardly dogs has been caught.

At the end of the platform some noise can be heard. The police are racing up the stairway, but the Commune is not too fond of this interference. A volley of bullets welcomes the officers. One bullet goes right through the shako[21] of the police captain, pushing it back until

---

[21] A tall stovepipe military hat worn by the Berlin Police.

it's dangling from his neck, held only by the strap.

The police take cover. The SA occupies all tracks. And then the SA and the police make a joint attack. Now the time has come. Nobody escapes. But before the Reds are handed over to the police, they get the SA treatment. One by one they are taken from their Compartment to receive their well-deserved beating. A proper one.

And now the SA-Men experience an odd spectacle. The Red Front men are on their knees in front of them, begging not to be hurt. They promise never, never, never to shoot again. Fearing for his life, one of them exclaims, "But we are just seduced workers!" The SA prick up their eyes at this desperate call. For a moment they may have thought that this wasn't entirely false, that it had some truth to it. But after today's events, they are left indifferent.

The Red Front men had a shawm [22] band with them. The instruments get shredded into a thousand pieces. One of the communists turns out to be Hoffmann [23], member of the state parliament. He receives some first-class slaps.

Then both the train and the station are searched. Pistols, ammunition, bullet casings, knives, revolvers, clubs, and brass knuckles. In the toilet, four guys are holed up, crying. One after another they are taken outside and beaten until tenderized.

A large crowd has gathered in front of the Lichterfelde station. When the Red Front men are taken away, the police can hardly protect them. Once again, they fear for their lives. The Berlin populace does not take kindly to cowardice.

Wounded SA-Men are carefully carried outside. Then the others form up into columns. But before they march off, Dr. Goebbels suddenly appears above their heads. His SA has spontaneously lifted him on their shoulders—a substantial, almost solemn gesture.

And the Doctor speaks. He speaks only a single breath, hard and cold, "SA-Men! We march to Berlin! Whoever opposes us, we will teach them about SA fists!"

The SA knows what these sentences mean. They answer with a single voice, a resounding, passionate cry. And then they march.

To both sides of the column marches the "Cotton." These are the civil stewards, who cover the brown train from the sidewalk. This

---

[22] An old-fashioned woodwind instrument similar in design to an oboe, but with a flared end similar to that of a trumpet.

[23] Paul Hoffmann, a German SPD and KPD politician and long-time parliamentarian during the Weimar Republic.

clever mechanism had been devised after the numerous assaults of recent times. These are strong, selected SA people in plain clothes. They do not wear any emblems or uniforms, but they're ready to step on the toes of anyone who looks suspicious, picks up a stone, or lets a hand wander towards their back pockets. They are men of steel and iron, with a reasonable ruthlessness. They march on the sidewalk next to their uniformed comrades, entirely unknown to the crowds cheering for the brown battalions. At most, a police report might mention fights between spectators during SA marches.

This is how the Cotton does its service.

On this bloody day, they are still doing their service. Today, the SA marches like a thundercloud. Almost threatening, almost silent. Marching without songs, without chants, without explanations. Only their flags are waving heavy and gloomy in the evening breeze. Today, a brooding aspect lies over these columns. Something is haunting their minds, rumbling inside their hearts, and it will not leave them in peace.

What did that communist yell in Lichterfelde-East? "But we are just seduced workers!"

This sentence occupies the SA during their silent march. Who is doing the actual seduction in this country? Who is constantly agitating in these lands? Who introduces one unrest after another to the German homeland?

The international Jew!

It came to them not by chance nor out of the blue, not as a dull, stubborn excuse, nor based on a childish view of life and the world in general. Nor was it due to intolerance, excited stupidity, or ignorance that this patient German people gradually began to feel a boundless hatred against the international Jew. As long as he went about his trade, as long as he worked like everyone else... fine. But then, after the war, he grew large, turned megalomaniacal and secretly usurped everything: politics, science, literature, theatre, film—all the things that make up the spirit of a country and its people. The SA does not consist of aesthetes. The SA consists of soldiers. And tonight, the SA strikes back for the first time.

From Kaiserplatz in Wilmersdorf to Wittenbergplatz, the Cotton treats every Jew it encounters with extreme unfriendliness.

The uniformed SA in the middle of the street does not even watch. That is none of their business. Their task is to carry the flag and the idea of Adolf Hitler through the West of Berlin, which is also called the Jewish West. At this moment it has to be nothing but the great threat of the Führer.

Many people disappear from Kurfürstendamm. Whoever is truly part of this country and this race does not even think of disappearing. Grimly the SA watches the wide street becoming increasingly empty.

The civil stewards make a small detour into the Romanisches Café.[24] They come across the gentlemen Münzenberg, Toller, Mühsam, Feuchtwanger, Kaestner, Loew, and Mandelbaum,[25] and if one of them should happen to be physically absent, their unclean spirits can still be seen sitting about. A little back and forth by the civil stewards is sufficient to empty this restaurant of everyone they don't want to see in here.

One window has been smashed, but it's not going to be the last. 314 cups of coffee were not paid for that day. They wouldn't have been paid for anyway. Then Goebbels speaks at Wittenbergplatz, and for the first time the deeply shocked West witnesses a National Socialist demonstration. It is also the first time they hear the Gauleiter of Berlin speak. After this speech, the SA disperses in a calm and disciplined manner.

But in their ears the shots from Lichterfelde-East are still echoing.

* * *

Schulz in his bunker has to be told about these events, because he was not there. First he glows with anger, then he burns with indignation, and finally he explodes. He ends up racing onto the street to buy newspapers, as many as he can carry and pay for. Then he broods over them with burning temples. Turning page after page, he looks up with a bewildered expression.

"Well?" they ask him mischievously. "They're all talking about Lichterfelde, right?"

Schulz turns page after page.

"Well?" they go on. "Everyone's outraged at the cowardly Red Front bunch, huh?"

Schulz reads:

---

[24] The Romanisches Café (Romanesque Café) was a well-known meeting spot in central Berlin, serving writers, actors and other creatives during the Weimar Republic. Many of its regulars were known to be Jewish.
[25] Ernst Toller and Erich Kaestner, among other persons listed here, were known to be frequent customers of the Romanesque Café.

"Pogrom in Berlin!"

"Hitler gangs hunt down defenseless Jews!"

"Brown murder spree on Kurfürstendamm!"

But try as he might, he can find only a single note on Lichterfelde-East: "Yesterday afternoon there were clashes at the Lichterfelde-East railway station between returning National Socialists and dissenters. Two participants were injured."

That's all Schulz finds, and everyone in the cellar laughs at his disappointed and angry face.

"Don't be so damned stupid," Karl finally says, "you should have known that the dogs would keep quiet about it."

Schulz gives no response. *The dogs,* he thinks, *these dogs!*

Propaganda tour of the Berlin SA, headed for the province.

Märkertag (Mark Day) of the Berlin SA.

9

SACRIFICE

April passes with little war and little of importance occurring in the world.

Only, in the SA cellar it came to pass that one evening, Karl Schindler strolls into the city and does not return. They stay up late, waiting for him. Then they spread out for a search. Schulz races through the streets like a tigress who has lost her cub. He and the boy Hermann search everywhere they can think of.

But Schulz was not meant to find his friend that night. When they return to the cellar in the morning, Ede is sitting there. He is pale and doesn't quite know what to say. Finally he comes out with it.

They have found Karl.

In Neukölln he lies, behind a wooden fence. Stuwe has stayed with him to wait for Schulz to come, and then Schulz is standing behind the fence. Karl is lying on his back, his arms wide open. In his frozen hands he still grips the red shreds of a communist poster.

Silently, Schulz kneels beside him, searching for the wound. Gently he rotates his body as if fearful of hurting him, and on his back he finds the wound. A broad, deep knife thrust has completely torn apart his lungs. On the ground there is a pool of blood.

"Killed from behind!" mumbles a perplexed Schulz. "Killed from behind!"

He doesn't even notice the tears streaming down his gaunt cheeks. Then he jumps up, absently looking at his silent comrades and rushes away. Hermann and Ede follow him.

Schulz comes back with a police man, who places a call to Alexanderplatz. Then some gentlemen arrive from there. Schulz demands a search for KPD members within the Hermannplatz precinct.

The detectives give him a chilly reply, emphasizing that this is their business, not his. For the time being there is no reason to call for such a search.

Distraught by his dead friend, the SA-Man Schulz throws himself at the useless detective.

He is immediately arrested and taken away.

In the evening he returns to the cellar.

No one dares to talk to him.

He begins to smooth out a board, three feet long, sixteen inches wide. He nails it to the cellar door and burns a cross into the top left corner, writing down the name of Karl Schindler next to it, along with the day and hour when they found him.

"There will be plenty of crosses to add." His voice is freezing cold. "War is not cheap. There will be sacrifice."

Then he hangs a small oak wreath around the cross.

10

MAY DAY

Then comes the 1st of May.

One of them has brought the news from headquarters, and within the SA joy and expectation have taken hold.

On the 1st of May Adolf Hitler wants to speak in the Reich capital for the very first time.

And it is the right day for such a man to speak in Berlin, exactly the right day: the great day of the SPD, the great day of the Internationale, the great day of Marxist hosts and their captains.

In the SA home, they talk about the meaning of May Day. They are well familiar with its meaning post 1918. But most of them are only now learning about this day's significance in the German past. The great joy of springtime, the great day of rebirth and reconstruction, leading up to the eternal struggle for life, the oldest celebration of sun and light within the Germanic race.

On this 1st of May, Adolf Hitler will speak in Berlin.

The assembly is set to take place in the Clou, a large hall in the city center.

That morning Schulz happens across a fleeting acquaintance on the street, with whom he would have gotten along quite well if it weren't for his SPD membership. And so they do not get along very well.

"You can talk all you want," says the socialist, "the street belongs to the proletariat and we won't let go of it, not for a single minute, no way. And the 1st of May belongs to us, the proletariat, as well, and we won't let go of that one either. This is a labor day, not a labor-murderer day, you get it? And the capitalists' mercenaries, the fascists—"

"You poor lunatic...," Schulz interrupts him, putting a calming hand on the socialist's arm. "No need for all that bombastic talk. Listen to me. You know that I'm a Nazi, don't you? And by now you should have noticed that for the past three months, the streets no longer belong to the socialists, but to us Nazis, right?"

"You are all provocateurs!" returns the socialist accusingly.

Schulz nods. He is not the slightest bit angry at this accusation. "But of course we are," he says cheerfully, "of course. Up till now you've been doing the provocation. Now we are provoking. That's the way of the world, isn't it? Yes, we are provoking intensely, you can bet on that. Do you still think we're some kind of bourgeois party? All Hurrahs and Victory against France? No, no, no, you've got it all backwards. Completely wrong."

The other one shrugs his shoulders. "You can never take May Day away from the proletariat."

Schulz smiles. "Let me tell you something," he says, "of course we will take the 1st of May away from the proletariat. And then we will return it to the German people; do you know what I mean?"

"Nope."

"Then let me tell you a little secret: One day there will no longer be a proletariat, just a German people, a people which no longer knows about class. Only people's comrades and so on. Do you at least understand that, you dumb bastard?"

And with that he leaves the red comrade, whistling as he goes on.

Nothing belongs to you, he thinks happily, *nothing at all.* Not the street and not the German worker. Not the state, not the economy, and not the 1st of May.

It will soon become apparent, Schulz continues to think, that all of this belongs to the SA. And the SA will only hand it over to the Führer. And the Führer ought to know what's to be done with it.

* * *

The assembly is packed. Never before has an NSDAP assembly been this overcrowded. In front of the Clou, crowds of people without a seat have gathered. And even out here they are fiercely defending their spot.

The Führer is coming. Never before have they seen the Führer; they have only heard and read about him. Now he, the soul of the party, its burning spirit, will appear here. They would prefer to be beaten to death rather than leaving this place.

The newspaper *Montag Morgen* is announced. It is teeming with scary headlines:

56

"Unprecedented provocation!"

"May Day clashes!"

"Hitler threatens!"

"Hitler's diatribe!"

The crowd waiting in front of the Clou looks up in surprise. Has Hitler already spoken? Have they been dreaming, or what's the deal with this newspaper?

The SA buys the salesman's entire stock. He can't help it if some higher-ups have been causing mischief.

And someone has definitely been causing mischief here!

A Jewish journalist reports on a Hitler meeting, which has yet to take place: "...Then Hitler spoke... he announced that Marxism... with demagogic impudence this Bavarian Pied Piper claimed..."

Amazed SA-Men turn the pages back and forth, reading these lines again and again. Never before have they experienced anything like this, and they have experienced a lot in the Reich capital.

They read a report about the whole meeting, completely thought up by a brash, lying scribe on Sunday morning.

Let the devil take him!

When the Führer arrives amidst whirlwinds of cheers and steps behind the lectern, he finds the newspaper lying there, neatly opened. An SA-Man has placed it there. As the Führer lets his gaze wander across the report, he understands the reasons behind the incessant hailing both inside and outside the hall.

He permits only a slight smile to pass over his face before he begins to speak.

And he speaks with all the deadly seriousness that burns inside him, all the vividness that makes his speeches resonate with even the simplest man, and all the boldness of a man who knows that his faith will never leave him.

11

JOURNALISTS

The press pounces on this man and his speech in the darkest, most hateful ways.

Never before have they amassed the sad courage to tell such lies, an unprecedented level of lying.

For the first time Dr. Goebbels is aghast with anger.

"We will show these gentlemen!" he shouts grimly. "We will put a stop to this brand of journalism. These press bandits who start their day with lies and go to sleep with slander, who invent conversations because they flew down the stairs when their impertinent visages dared to demand an interview. Who vengefully insult Adolf Hitler as a drunkard and deadbeat, because he did not wish to engage with these pompous fools. One day we will set these gentlemen straight! Not today and not tomorrow but one day..."

"What?!" he asks them and laughs again, his strangely youthful laugh, which all of a sudden has taken on a dangerous and fateful look.

"One day!"

"We want to have a meeting!" exclaims the Doctor. "Yesterday was the 1st, today is the 2nd, the day after tomorrow, on the 4th of May there will be a meeting at the veteran's association! Topic: The press and its reporting!"

He has barely expressed this thought, before his pen starts flying over the paper. He is already in the process of drafting the proclamation for this meeting.

The following morning posters have been put up on all corners and fences. Berlin nervously shakes its collective head.

What is the matter with this fellow who won't give them even a moment's rest? Just three days ago there was a huge meeting, and now he's calling for another one?

Devil take him, does he think that Berlin has nothing else to do but go to his meetings?

Let him see how few people will attend this time! And besides, does he want to mess around with the press? With the all-powerful Berlin press, whom no one has ever been able to match?

Very well, then he will learn his lesson.

But on the other hand, Berlin can't resist a smile.

Gradually they have come to know the Doctor, the SA and the party, and they wouldn't put it past them to pull off something like this.

There is a tremendous atmosphere in the Storm pub.

"It will be thi-i-i-i-s full!" Hermann yells, clenching his fists tightly together to show how packed the room would become and that nobody would be able to move in the crowd.

"It will be!" the others yell back, and everyone is full of confidence.

* * *

"They won't be able to scrape together even three hundred men," editor Dembitzer of the *Mittag Zeitung* calls his local manager, "but we must be bold about it. Take three people with you! No, take even more! Have them work in shifts! Note down everything in shorthand! I want to know exactly what this Goebbels has to say about the press! Come over here for a second."

Then Dembitzer races through the room and suddenly stops. He stares at his local manager. "You know what?" he asks, playing with his pencil, "just send three Blondes there."

Mr. Dembitzer has invented the funny nickname "Blondes" for the Christians among the editorial staff. Especially the reporters.

* * *

"You think we'll have a proper brawl again?" asks Hermann.

"Nonsense," explains Schulz, who has gradually become an expert on questions of brawling, "why should there be trouble?"

"There's always trouble," remarks Hermann philosophically, grinning.

* * *

Dembitzer gives his orders. "Call in... go to the nearest cigarette store... call in: Incidents, if anything's happening. Especially incidents. Hopefully it stays empty."

* * *

But it does not stay empty. One and a half hours before the beginning of the meeting one couldn't even let a pin drop, and half an hour later the crowd becomes life threatening.

Those who have just arrived can no longer enter the hall.

It has been closed down by the police. Hermann rejoices loudly. The hall really has become thi-i-i-i-s full. It had happened just like he predicted, and surely there would be trouble as well.

But so far, everything remains quiet.

There is no roaring and jeering crowd. There are no beer glasses shattering on the wall, no chair legs being swung.

Instead there is a thunderstorm of enthusiasm and a typhoon of indignation in the hall.

Dr. Goebbels ruthlessly settles accounts with the press. He goes directly for the throat of the ruling system's journalists. The hall rages. Even the well-disciplined and well-behaved SA, who is never allowed to interfere, to clap their hands or simply participate in any statements of the assemblies, even this SA, moved by bitterness and indignation, forgets all education and cannot help but shout along, cheer, and clap their hands.

And then Dr. Goebbels comes to the end. Everyone can feel that the final reckoning is about to commence.

The hall is feverish.

At this moment, a drunk individual rises from a table near the front of the hall, completely smashed. And just as the Doctor begins to speak of the foreign-born newspaper writers, he cries up to the lectern, "You don't look so good yourself!"

The assembly freezes.

It is obvious that this lout is not a communist.

This is no opponent at all, just a simple drunk.

And that's also exactly what Schulz thinks.

He doesn't consider this interjection particularly severe, but nevertheless he will make sure that this guy can't blurt out another one. And before any order can reach him, he moves towards the table.

He just barely notices Dr. Goebbels addressing the troublemaker in a manner that seems both mildly surprised and somewhat paternalistic.

"Do you intend to disturb the meeting?" the Doctor asks quite peacefully. "Perhaps you would like us to take you outside for a breath of fresh air?"

But of course he would like that, Schulz thinks and works his way further towards the table, *he would definitely like that.*

Now he has reached the troublemaker's table, but just then, the drunkard once again shouts an incomprehensible sentence into the hall.

Stupid bastard, thinks Schulz, *why can't you just shut it?*

And to prevent any further interference, Schulz gives the individual a few medium slaps, left and right, dissipating a heavy smell of alcohol in a mile-wide radius. Then he picks up the lush and calmly carries him through the hall and out of the door, surrounded by laughter and applause from the crowd.

The rally continues calmly.

Soon everyone has forgotten about the heckler.

The Doctor once again commences his final reckoning. It has become quiet in the hall, except for raging applause every now and then.

Suddenly there is another interruption.

The crowd near the entrance grows restless, and voices can be heard.

One can see shakos and uniforms appearing.

The police!

What do the police want here! Is the meeting not peaceful?

Why are the police making such a racket?

All of a sudden, it has become impossible to understand the Doctor.

Quiet! Quiet! Get the police to leave!

A shrill whistle blows through the hall, and now an unprecedented howling begins. An immense downpour of whistles greets the guardians of republican order.

One can see a police officer climbing onto the podium.

"Silence!" he yells. "The assembly will be searched for weapons!"

The crowd answers him with roaring laughter.

Just about the right time for a joke like that.

Great, excellent!

And now the Berliners start talking to their policeman.

"Come on over here, lad, I'm the one!"

"Take a look, I've got a cannon down my pants!"

"Officer! I've got a flamethrower in my pockets! Careful please!"

"Officer, are toothpicks a criminal offence?"

The cops are getting a little red in the face. Silently they search the people, one after another.

SA-jokes are hailing down on them, and these SA-jokes are not for sensitive and delicate natures. Fortunately these policemen are not particularly sensitive or delicate themselves.

For two hours the meeting allows itself to be examined, having a tremendous amount of fun. As time goes by, the police are no longer enjoying the affair, because there are zero results.

No rifle, no knife, no broken tree branches or fence poles, not even some harmless brass knuckles. And eventually they leave again.

The meeting is over.

It ended long after midnight.

A royal delight for the SA.

"Was I right or was I right?" shouts a cheerful Schulz. "No trouble, no brawl, no nothing. Things are looking up!"

"Let's drink to that," suggests Edc.

"Sure," says Schulz, "lots of nice, pale ales. A dime each."

As they treat themselves to their pints, they get increasingly jolly. Only Hermann is not in a particularly good mood.

He predicted a hall fight, and personally he would have preferred a proper brawl. An opinion which he expresses unapologetically.

Schulz lets out a long sigh.

"That's youth," he says, shaking his head, "nothing but a big mouth and always up for a fight. A battle is all right if it has to be. But if you can avoid it, you're better off without a hole in your head and dead as a doornail. Because once you're dead, that's final. You're not coming back from that. So it's better without a battle."

The SA is extremely satisfied with this assembly, and so is Dr. Goebbels.

*　*　*

Until the next day arrives.

That day, everything is different.

On this day the newspapers reported that the SA had attacked a clergyman, brutally beating up an ordained priest, an inhuman maltreatment.

The SA is dumbfounded, left to scratch its collective head. The Doctor's mouth grows extremely narrow.

"Was there a priest in the assembly?" he asks briefly.

The adjutant clicks his heels.

"I didn't see anyone."

"Did you read the papers?"

"Affirmative!"

The Doctor ponders this question.

These are grave accusations, and the party's dignity demands immediate action.

"So you didn't see a clergyman being maltreated? A priest beaten up? Good heavens, do they take us for idiots!"

His face turns deep red with indignation.

"I want to know what's going on! Those lying Journalists!" Then he calmly adds, "Find out exactly what happened. And then immediately issue a denial. Paragraph 11."

The Berlin SA is searched for weapons by the Bernau police.

12

Outlaws

The brave SA-Men of Berlin are dumbfounded. They have heated debates in Storm pubs and offices, at unemployment offices and on the job.

They have no clue what's going on. People are saying that they've beaten up a priest? They're supposed to be such pigs who would attack a servant of God?

And so a tremendous question and answer session commences throughout the SA. The SA investigates itself, and man for man examines the entire stupid story.

Nobody has seen anything. Nobody has noticed anything. Nobody has seen even the slightest glimpse of a priest.

Schulz is also thinking hard about this, but comes up empty. The only thing that he and the others can remember was that affair with the drunkard.

And as they think back and forth, a terrible suspicion overcomes Schulz.

"Gee," he says hoarsely, "what if that drunken pig was a priest?"

They look at him like he's crazy.

And then Schulz is called to the Doctor. There he reports what actually happened to the drunk at that meeting. He makes his report clear and simple, like he did a thousand times on the Western Front.

The Doctor remembers the incident very well. Schulz receives no reproach whatsoever. He did not make the slightest mistake, he only did his duty, and the Doctor knows that's all there is to it. He shakes hands with Schulz, exchanging many friendly words with him. And then he starts to think about how to remedy this poisonous dart.

Because the press now has a potentially fatal talking point. Then police headquarters decide to start an official investigation. News reporting about the incident is accelerating, rumors are getting thicker and thicker, every new issue of every newspaper has a new factoid to add.

And before twenty-four hours are up, National Socialists are considered dangerous beasts that must be exterminated or at the very least locked up all together. Either way, under no circumstance should any of them be allowed to roam freely through the streets of Berlin.

It won't be long before they become even more vicious and dangerous, until the Reich capital suffocates in blood and murder.

Didn't they shoot at defenceless workers at Lichterfelde-East?

Didn't they stage a wild pogrom on Kurfürstendamm?

They are capable of anything and everything, so what does the police intend to do against them? The press knows very well how to formulate its questions and demands.

Like this: "Does a priest have to be beaten to death before the authorities finally see reason?"

As it turned out, this little man who got carried outside by Schulz had no longer been a priest anyway. And he certainly hadn't been beaten to death, even though he promptly wrapped some gauze bandages around his head to underline his bragging.

The press did not take notice of this.

In fact, the *Berliner Zeitung* was way too busy announcing an imminent ban of the Berlin NSDAP the very next day.

"Oh dammit," Schulz said dejectedly, "now it's getting serious. How do the newspaper people know about the ban?"

And then he slams his fist on the table, loud enough to make the others jump up in horror.

"What's the matter?" they yell at him.

And he yells back. "What's the matter? So you hit a drunkard in the face, and all of a sudden the party is gone. That's what's up."

He gives his friends a miserable look and they return an equally dismal one.

So this is how things were to end?

The top cellar of the Third Reich, Storm pub, home for the boys... finished, done for, busted.

Slowly, very slowly they begin to understand the power of the press, something that had completely eluded their imagination up till now.

And gradually these SA-Men are also beginning to understand that behind these powers of press and police, there must be something else, something vague and shifty, a secret power that is now squaring up against them, working towards their destruction.

They were unable to say what exactly it was, but even in those days they already smelled it, they felt it, and with a painful clarity they suddenly understood the tremendous struggle which they were part of. The struggle that also involved the Führer Adolf Hitler, the Doctor, and a great many others who were of their spirit. Thinking of the Führer, Schulz breathes a sigh of relief.

"Man, one day we will win after all," he says to Hermann, "but whether I'll live to see it, I dunno. It's bound to take a long damn time. You know Isidor, he's still giving us a hard time. Isidor, vice police commissioner. If it was just him... who cares? Great publicity in fact. But all of the other Isidors behind him..."

Schulz looks around the home they have built together, the beds, the curtains, the floor, the stove...

It had been a very good time in here...

Hermann lets his friend talk and growl, but says nothing. He is young and doesn't really believe in the difficulties that are still to come. He is not a field soldier and does not yet have an instinct for trouble. To him, all of this was just a bunch of hollow words.

But the others are taking it very seriously.

That night they dissolve their home.

The beds go to Fritz. The linoleum on the floor comes to Hermann. He also agrees to store the stove.

Schulz goes with Ede, who takes the table and one of the chairs. They distribute the other chair and another old armchair among the others, together with the card games, the chess set, the lamp, their books and pictures.

Finally, SA-Man Schulz wraps the large swastika flag around his body.

Hermann gets to carry the wooden board with the burnt-in crosses and the name of Karl Schindler written on it. Then they take another look at the bare room. It looks just as desolate as the first day Karl discovered it. Before they leave, they prepare to have a bit of fun with their persecutors.

Writing on a sheet of brown wrapping paper, they compose a final verse, a verse for the police when they come to sniff around the place. They place this sheet in the middle of the empty room, so that everyone who enters has to notice it right away:

Die Vöglein sind schon ausgeflogen	*The birds have already flown away.*
Umsonst hast du dich aufgerogen,	*You've got yourself all worked up for*
Isidor!	*nothing, Isidor!*
Doch einmal,	*But one day,*
Wenn wir wiederkommen,	*When we come back,*
Dann wirst du kräftig hopp	*We'll have a little fun with you,*
Genommen, Isidor!	*Isidor!*
Verbieten kannst du nicht den Geist,	*You cannot forbid the spirit,*
Was schlagend dieses Lied beweist.	*We aptly proved it with this song.*
Heil Hitler!	*Heil Hitler!*

They come out onto the street. At this hour, it lies silent and deserted. Only at the corner they can see the shako of a policeman. Suddenly a roaring "Hail Victory!" tears through the night air, causing the jumpy policeman to turn about abruptly. Some figures appear in the windows, trying to see what this commotion is all about.

The SA makes a quick retreat—the Commune is particularly uncomfortable when they are frightened out of their sleep.

And so are the cops.

13

Return

The NSDAP and all of its sub-organizations have been banned for the Berlin area and the Brandenburg province. Signed Weiss, police commissioner of Berlin.

Terminates the party.

Terminates the SA.

Finally, thank God, the editorial offices are rejoicing. Now that the SA people have disappeared from the streets, they can focus on taking down a single man, Dr. Goebbels.

But this undertaking of theirs should turn out to be quite a bit harder than they imagined...

The Jew Bernhard Weiss,[26] nicknamed Isidor, banned the SA? Because some of his Eastern racial comrades had received a few crooked looks on Kurfürstendamm?

Because of that? Because of that?

No, gentlemen, that is not a proper reason to all of a sudden ban the SA and NSDAP.

Editor Dembitzer dictates: "It is to be assumed that the person solely responsible for these scandalous events, Gauleiter Goebbels, will be arrested within the coming days. There is grave evidence that he not only called for trespassing, but also personally participated in preparations for treason. Above all, he has accrued a most severe moral guilt—the guilt for the blood of the innocents, spilt by his unholy SA-Men."

"Have it typeset immediately. I want to proofread the manuscript right away," Dembitzer says to the messenger boy who delivers

---

[26] An active member of the Jewish community in Berlin and vice president of the Berlin Police from 1927 to 1932. He was a frequent target of caricaturists. In 1933 an arrest warrant was issued for him by the National Socialist government. Weiss narrowly escaped to Prague and then London, where he died in 1951.

manuscripts to the typesetting department.

Dembitzer is in a particularly foul mood.

"Stop!" he shouts after the messenger, "the headline!"

He adds some large, bold letters to his manuscript: "Upcoming arrest of Dr. Goebbels?"

Soon the newspapers begin to carry small notes, spiteful and malicious.

"Is Goebbels fleeing to Upper Silesia?" asks the *Mittag Zeitung*.

And then it claims that the Berlin Gauleiter wants to escape, abandoning his seduced following, that he even wants to abandon his SA, who are starting to file into prisons at his behest.

"Look," calls the yellow press, "that's your leader in Berlin! As soon as something goes wrong, he runs away, leaving you in the dirt."

But despite these efforts, the gentlemen of high politics within the press become increasingly nervous when they receive one of their requested reports. What does the SA think about their Doctor? The gentlemen wished to know.

Well, the SA laughs.

So naturally they want to make sure the SA won't be laughing very long. Again these notes appear, both small and large:

"Adolf Hitler showered Dr. Goebbels with grave accusations!"

"Serious disagreements between the dictator in Munich and his Berlin Gauleiter!"

"Chief bandit finally fallen from grace!"

"Goebbels to be transferred to new post!"

What does the Berlin SA say to that?

The SA is still laughing.

They do not believe it.

As a matter of fact, they say that it's nothing but a damned press swindle, and the SA goes on to say that they are well aware of the lying press.

In the cafés, and salons, in the editorial offices, circles, cliques, and conventions, certain gentlemen are beside themselves at the thought of there being someone in Berlin who does not believe the press.

* * *

One day Mr. Dembitzer sweats with delight. Unfortunately, there are many such Dembitzers in the press, far too many. And the SA gets to know these Dembitzers all too well.

Mr. Dembitzer has received a wonderful message.

Goebbels is traveling to Stuttgart!

The Jewish gentlemen in the press are rejoicing, and they aren't shy about it. From the very first day of the NSDAP's struggle to gain ground in Berlin, they recognized them as an immense danger for themselves. They certainly did not underestimate this danger.

An hour later after Dembitzer received his wonderful news, the rotary press spits out sheet after sheet, each with a large headline.

"Goebbels fled to Stuttgart!"

"Upcoming arrest of Goebbels?"

"Will Goebbels cross the border?"

"Goebbels abandons his followers!"

* * *

Even the SA-Man Schulz buys one of those fresh papers. And reads. And gives Hermann a nudge, maybe a little too hard.

"Ouch, damn it!" he shouts. "What..."

"Shut it!" says Schulz, "Straighten out and listen. Can you figure out when the Doctor will be back from Stuttgart? Because then we could come and pick him up, you know? And he's never been picked up like that before, if you know what I mean."

Hermann is amazed.

"Man," he stutters, "that's a great idea, I–"

"Quiet!" says Schulz, "and keep it secret, Hermann!"

"Secret, on my honor!"

And the two SA-Men, who should actually be banned, go on the prowl. They do not rest until they have learned exactly when a certain express train with a certain man on it will arrive at a certain Berlin station.

Two days later, a remarkable amount of people stroll around Königgrätzer Straße. They seem to have plenty of time. For a while they stand around in front of Hotel Excelsior, languidly inspecting the entrance, complete with a few modest jokes about the porter. Then they stroll past Anhalter station to look at the arriving cabs, before they proceed to saunter towards Möckernstraße and sections of Anhaltstraße.

Eventually there are more and more of these people. Strolling about, nodding and shouting cheerful words among themselves. As darkness sets in it, thousands and thousands of them are standing on

Askanischer Platz, and still more are arriving. Whole clusters of people jump off the arriving trams and buses. Gradually, the two policemen stationed on the square become a bit nervous.

What is going on here?

In any case, they will call the precinct and prepare accordingly, although the crowd that has gathered gives them no reason for actual concern.

They are not shouting and hollering, no one is giving a speech or waving a flag, they are almost silent, as if they were waiting for something very specific to occur.

* * *

But suddenly, as if lightning had struck, silence and tranquillity come to an end. As if from a single throat, an immense scream breaks loose against the station building. And this scream breaks down into a thousand shouts.

One man has stepped out of the station and looked around, and before he can finish his survey, four fists have grabbed him and lifted him up on their shoulders so that everyone can see him.

He raises his hand in salute, receiving an artillery fire of "Heils" in response. And this fire can be heard as far as Potsdamer Platz and Hallesches Tor, a cry of devotion, anger, love, and threat.

What is happening? The Nazis are picking up their "escaped" Goebbels from Anhalter Bahnhof—that's all there is to it.

But isn't that reason enough?

The Doctor is back!

The Nazis are overjoyed that the Doctor is back, and their joy reaches such levels of excitement that the policemen lose their nerve and quickly make another phone call to the precinct.

With howling sirens the riot squad arrives.

Dear God, let them come.

Then the SA-Man Schulz pumps his two lungs full of as much air as he can manage and shouts a verse into the crowd, a very short one, but it is understood, "Despite the ban—not dead!"

Some SA comrades near him consider this verse impeccably short and more than ready for use. They yell it again; then more and more people on the square join in until finally the whole crowd is yelling it.

"What are they shouting?" a young police officer asks the constable standing next to him; both of them have lowered their chinstraps and

71

their hands are holding rubber truncheons. The constable explains.

The younger officer looks at the man for a brief moment; then both of them grin. They are not allowed to say what that grin was all about, but if in a few minutes they should receive the order to strike, these two will use their rubber truncheons only to keep up appearances.

14

CHICANERY

People in the street stop and turn around.

What is this?

Truly, an impudence beyond belief!

The squares and bourgeois lean out of the windows, staring down in indignation. Young lads with the Soviet star on their chest stop and turn bright red with rage. The policeman directing the traffic forgets to regulate it for a full minute, unsure whether he is supposed to draw his pistol in cases such as this.

Someone is marching across the street... with a brown shirt... in plain trousers, but with a brown shirt!

And there is another one marching with a brown shirt.

And yet another one wearing a brown shirt under his jacket.

That has to count as provocation!

A downright mockery of the state even! Finally a policeman who isn't busy regulating traffic turns the corner and picks out one of these impertinent blokes.

"Hey, you there..."

The brown shirt stops. Pulling an exceedingly stupid face, he looks up at the officer in amazement. "What is it, Officer?"

"Take that shirt off!"

The one in the brown shirt opens his eyes wide. "Well now, Constable! Here, in front of all the ladies? But Officer..."

"Man," growls the officer, "that's a Nazi shirt, isn't it?"

This seems to amaze the bloke. "A Nazi shirt? This one? Why, Officer! That's my unemployment shirt, my private shirt! Completely and utterly private! And it wasn't even brown to begin with...," here the boy looks around to make sure everyone is listening, and then he tiptoes towards the officer's hairy left ear, whispering loud enough for the whole street to hear, "...it wasn't even brown to begin with, that's just the way it looks because we're constantly getting shat on by the higher-ups."

And then he storms off as fast as he can. The policeman's jaw audibly drops, but before he can enact appropriate punitive measures, there is no-one left to receive them.

There is tremendous grinning among the audience.

The constable is furious.

"Move on!" he snaps.

That's all he can do.

* * *

Once again an NSDAP poster emblazons the columns.

Dr. Goebbels speaks on the topic: "A life of beauty and dignity."

The party may have been banned, but elections are upcoming in Prussia, and they were guaranteed to be free elections. Naturally, free elections include assemblies, and so Dr. Goebbels will hold a meeting.

The gentlemen at the Alexanderplatz precinct are pulling sour faces. Again and again they read the topic Dr. Goebbels wants to talk about, and their faces are getting increasingly sour. This rabid Nazi wants to talk about a life of beauty and dignity?

This is going to be yet another one of his underhanded moves.

They are beginning to understand his strategy.

And once again the unequivocally fair newspapers run their sensible bold headlines: "Goebbels banned from speaking?"

The SA has been very patient so far, even for their thick-skinned standards, but now their patience is running out.

Already an assembly of state parliament member Haake has been banned, so the SA would like to show that they're still alive and that they are fully aware of the people pulling strings behind the scenes.

Suddenly, Kurfürstendamm is visited by twenty rough figures. Each Eastern Jew passing by gets treated rather rudely and receives some pretty unfriendly looks.

Alarm bells ring incessantly at the local precinct, and then riot squads come speeding along in their speedy cars, speeding upwards and downwards, starting the hunt.

Anyone wearing anything even remotely resembling a windbreaker or an even slightly brown shirt is arrested and loaded onto police trucks.

The posh avenue brims with vigorous shouting.

But they also have a lot of fun where the trucks are parked, because the arrestees are excitedly pelting their surroundings with witty commentary.

"Faster, gentlemen, faster!"

"Customers in the shop, gentlemen, customers in the shop!"

"Let's have a little hunt!"

And then suddenly the packed trucks are resounding with beautiful old German folk songs.

<table>
<tr><td>Ein Jäger aus der Kurpfalz</td><td>A hunter of Kurpfalz</td></tr>
<tr><td>Der reitet durch den grünen Wald;</td><td>Is riding through the green woods;</td></tr>
<tr><td>Er reitet hin und her,</td><td>He shoots the wild game,</td></tr>
<tr><td>So wie es ihm gefällt.</td><td>Just the way he likes it best.</td></tr>
<tr><td>Gar lustig ist die Jägerei,</td><td>How good it is to go hunting,</td></tr>
<tr><td>Allhier auf grüner Heid,</td><td>All over the green fields,</td></tr>
<tr><td>Allhier auf grüner Heid.</td><td>All over the green fields.</td></tr>
</table>

Surely they are still allowed to sing, right? Surely no-one would want to ban singing German folk songs?

* * *

Oh yes. That's life right now.

One day the ban on the province of Brandenburg has to be lifted. As it turns out, the Berlin police do not have the authority to issue a ban for the whole of Brandenburg.

Well, the police are creative enough to help themselves.

In Berlin, they are banning the Schlageter celebration.[27]

Allegedly celebrations in memory of this man run the risk of "disturbing peace and order."

"Well then," says SA-Man Schulz as he sets off to visit some of the small, cozy clubs of which he has become a member.

The Thursday Club, Alt-Berlin, Ball Sports Club. He stalks towards Father Kunz in Landsberger Straße and South-West Sports in Katzbachstraße.

Gradually, the SA-Man Schulz has built an impressive knowledge of the Berlin club life.

---

[27] Albert Schlageter was a German Freikorps fighter who was executed in 1923 after sabotaging a railway track in the French-occupied Ruhr region, the industrial heartland of Germany.

Recently a whole bunch of small new clubs have been founded. Schulz could recite their addresses, telephone numbers, and membership lists in his dreams.

Before leaving he once again takes his Iron Cross from a drawer.

Looking at it, it doesn't feel quite as shiny as when the battalion commander awarded it to him, wrapped in blue paper, so Schulz cleans it up a bit.

And then he recalls the Kemmel; he thinks of Cyprus, the Somme, and the Argonne Forest. He thinks of the great American attack in which herds of masked animals on both sides slaughtered each other. When the enemies removed their gas masks, thick, red-cheeked, healthy faces appeared. But on his side of the trench, Schulz witnessed nothing but pale, gaunt, hollowed-out faces, the collective face of the German soldier in 1918, this almost supernatural miracle of toughness, bravery, and loyalty unto death.

Schulz wipes his forehead.

A lot of time has passed since then. And God willing, all of this shall bear fruit one day. Until now it certainly did not look that way. All these dead children of their fatherland... would their sacrifice have meaning after all?

His lips pressed tightly together. Schulz polishes the Iron Cross until it won't get any brighter. Then he pins the medal on his brown shirt.

Later on, a few hundred brown shirts are casually marching through the streets of Berlin. They do not march in lock step, because they know they're actually forbidden and they know to give the devil his due.

They are just strolling to a meeting.

And they wear brown shirts because they are unemployed and that one brown shirt is all they have. They simply cannot buy another.

But the policemen seem entirely unconvinced by this line of argument. They simply strip them off their shirts, those dangerous subversive shirts, until Schulz and his friends are left shirtless, completely bare chested but calm, happy, and not very upset at all. Then all of them are loaded onto a single truck.

Where to? To Alexanderplatz of course.

Schulz looks at his Iron Cross, which he has taken off his shirt and is now holding in his hand.

Then he takes a roll of leucoplast out of his old army trousers. He always carries it with him, so he can play paramedic for his friends in case of the little emergencies that tend to accompany SA duty.

Now he tears off a strip and neatly fixes the Iron Cross on his bare chest. The constable sitting between them looks at this undertaking with a grin.

"Now let's go," Schulz says calmly, "are we going for a ride in the countryside? Little bit of sun? So we can get a nice brown tan on the outside as well? We're already brown on the inside, officer."

The SA-Man Schulz considers this to be a short episode. He has yet to realize just how often he will have to tape the Iron Cross to his chest in the future.

Because the struggle has only just begun.

15

Attack

A rumor starts to make the rounds in late June.

The party will get a newspaper, an actual weekly paper for the Doctor to express his thoughts as often as he wants and in whatever form he wants. "A newspaper?" says the SA, "that's expensive." And they are a little hesitant, because neither the Doctor nor the SA has any money.

"Whatever," Schulz confidently says, "no newspapers without money. Sure, I get it. But if the Doctor wants to have a newspaper, then he creates one. So he creates one without money."

And so it happened. The Doctor creates a newspaper without money. Once again the SA got it right. The paper was founded on two thousand marks. Only the Doctor and a few confidants knew about this ridiculous amount, a thoroughly impossible sum.

At first nobody had any idea what the paper would be called, but the news travel fast regardless: The Berlin NSDAP gets its own newspaper!

On the 1st of July the advertising columns are covered by large posters, showing nothing but a giant question mark. And Berlin curiously examines this question mark. Now what's that supposed to mean?

A new cigarette? Cleaning agent? A new novel in the *Münchner Illustrierte*? A new theatre performance or a new film?

Even many party comrades take puzzled looks at this mysterious question mark.

On the 2nd of July the poster reads: "Attack!"

And underneath it again the question mark.

Attack? What do they mean, Attack?

What's "Attack" supposed to mean, Berlin asks without even the slightest clue. Only the Berlin SA has a slight hunch, which they enthusiastically discuss among themselves.

And on the third day, the 3rd of July, the question mark has disappeared and the poster announces:

The Attack[28]
The German weekly newspaper in Berlin!
Publisher: Dr. Goebbels

So that's what it was all about! Berlin is a little perplexed.

The SA is cheering.

And on Monday, July 4th, 1927, SA-Man Schulz stands at the corner of Friedrichstraße and Zimmerstraße, shouting in his best and loudest voice, *"The Attack!* The German Monday paper! The paper of our German Berlin! The paper by Dr. Goebbels! *The Attack! The Attack!"*

Just like him, many SA-Men adopted this new duty and this new battle cry. Overnight, they have become newsagents, and the name of this new paper simply rolls off their tongue.

---

[28] German title: *Der Angriff*

16

NUREMBERG

But Berlin has not yet been conquered.

And even though Schulz and many of his comrades are standing on street corners to proclaim their newspaper, results are still rather poor.

The SA-Man Schulz sees many future party comrades passing him by. In vain he stretches his newspaper out to them.

Damn it all! And then the eternal claptrap in the clubs... was this how the Third Reich should come about?

Their work is harder than ever. The vice police commissioner, little Isidor, has posted sharp lookouts and sharp guards.

Things have reached the point where one has little choice but to sneak through empty streets in the dead of night, secretly putting up a few posters with hasty slaps of glue. Or to race from building to building, rapidly shoving leaflets into mail slots.

That's all, and under such circumstances it's already a lot. Their brown uniform stays hidden in the closet as summer passes them by.

The boys are meeting at Father Mehl's[29] place. Father Mehl is a pavement setter and has been unemployed for a long time. His skull is wonderfully square with short grey hair, and his wide hands are calloused and very slow in their movements. For thirty-five years these hands have worked. Now they are forced to rest senselessly.

Father Mehl is a widower. His wife died in the Turnip Winter.[30] At

---

[29] The term "Father" was used more widely in the past and did not refer exclusively to family relations or priests. It is likely that Bade chose to create Father Mehl as a mix between a general father/grandfather figure, using "Father" as a term of endearment and a way to demonstrate the close emotional bond between different generations of Germans.
[30] The Turnip Winter of 1916–17 was caused by the combination of the British naval blockade of Germany during the First World War and an exceptionally poor potato harvest. This period of near-starvation caused a sharp increase in female mortality. Turnips, a root vegetable typically used for animal feed, were the only remaining food source for many

that time he was stationed in the Lausechampagne. He never saw her again. One of his sons immigrated to Canada; the other one disappeared in Upper Silesia. Perhaps Polish archives would have been able to provide some information about the missing person. Father Mehl's entire being is centered around taking care of people. And because he has no one left to care for, he just takes care of his SA lads instead, the seven SA-Men from the former top cellar.

He picked them up in a distillery once, sitting about homeless and slightly depressed. He immediately liked all seven of them, and since the feeling was mutual, everyone was fine with that.

Once the ban gets lifted, Father Mehl will become SA-Man Mehl.

And in the meantime, he plays hostel warden for the lads.

Now they are in the process of carefully dressing up for Nuremberg. For the party convention! The thought of getting to see the Führer face to face again, to hear his voice and feel the flames of passion radiating around him, this thought fills every single one of them with immense joy.

Those who did not yet know him when he first spoke in Berlin remained silent after this experience. For how could they express this deep emotion, the burning love for this man who walked towards destiny with deathly seriousness, sweeping along anyone worthy of his leadership.

Hitler!

What a living contradiction this man was.

All the hatred, slander, infamy, lies, and derision, all the spit and insults heaped on this man by his enemies. How different it was from the respect and affection he garnered, the tremendous love, loyalty, and trust that was put into him. The devotion and even faith he inspired in his own people.

Hitler!

Like a concentrated flame, his deadly seriousness burned everything he hated to cinders. And he hated everything that was not German, everything lukewarm, everything soft and lame.

Listening to his speeches, even the simplest of men understood his meaning, so tremendous were their power and vividness.

His speeches were not flowery and ornate. He did not address intellectuals, but reached out to all simple people. His speeches never felt artificial. They were an elementary force—not "maybe," but

---

Germans during this time.

"either-or!" When he said yes, he meant yes, and when he said no, he meant no. The purity of this character stood out in this rotten time like a bright torch against a blurry twilight.

The cleanliness of his private life was unimpeachable, beyond doubt. A strange, but uplifting case in these sultry and depraved times.

Many who went to hear him were perplexed by his harsh and ruthless language. Many trembled, believing that this man would surely bring about the civil war everyone dreaded.

But those who decided to put their faith in him remained undeterred. Among them the small group of SA-Men, who have gathered at Father Mehl's place to dress up for Nuremberg.

Nuremberg!

The Party and the SA may have been banned in Berlin. But the Berlin SA and SS are headed to Nuremberg for the party conference. That is not just right and proper; it simply has to be that way. Didn't the Führer order the Berlin SS to secure the event? Isn't the Berlin SA supposed to open the grand parade? Well then!

Their going to Nuremberg is obvious. Now all they have to figure out is how to get there. As it turns out, this question is still giving them some headaches.

At least they still have their "voters' associations."

"First of all," says Franz confidently, "we have a special train."

"Special train does sound nice. Question is, can we get on that train?"

Yes, indeed, that is the question.

Who's paying for this special train? The Party? Their outlawed party? That's a good one. The Party is in so much debt, it makes their heads spin. The Party lives on alms. Maybe the SA could pay for the special train? Let's have a closer look at that SA: Unemployed people, schoolchildren, working students, part-time workers... no, there's no money to be collected here.

Schulz can't stop scratching his head. Ever since they started thinking about this, his forehead has turned into a wrinkled mess.

And what a mess it is: Despite their fanatic thrift and despite the Storm's painful collective abstinence from beer, cigarettes, and sometimes even hot lunches, despite all of their savings... they are still short twenty Reichsmarks.

Father Mehl listens to the moaning until finally he has had enough of their lamentations.

"Shut up already," he says, pulling an ancient blue handkerchief from the very back of a cupboard. The Storm watches him indifferently as he carefully unties the old handkerchief. Then Father Mehl neatly unfolds its four blue corners, and what emerges from it? A twenty-mark piece, a real, golden twenty-mark piece from the pre-war period, brilliant and heavy.

The SA Storm freezes in silence and awe. Schulz grasps the gold piece, weighing it in his hand.

"Keep it," says Father Mehl, whose voice has taken on a hoarse tone, "doesn't matter if I have that one in my handkerchief or not, who cares."

None of the boys dare to say anything. They know full well that this fairy-tale of a coin is Father Mehl's last reserve, the very last. They know exactly what this sacrifice is worth.

The wrinkles on Schulz' forehead grow even deeper.

It is impossible to reject the gift. He is too deeply moved for many words, but something has to be said or done, otherwise their hearts might burst.

And suddenly Schulz walks almost menacingly towards Father Mehl, who makes a startled retreat. The Storm does not quite know what to make of this, until Schulz throws his arms around the old man, pressing him to his heart.

Then he pockets the twenty marks, and there is no more talk of it.

After they have said their goodbyes for the evening and are back on the street, Schulz asks, "It's a matter of honor that Father Mehl gets his twenty marks back, right?"

"And if we have to stay sober for a whole year, we'll pay him back." replies another. That settles the matter.

They are scheduled to leave the next day.

Again they have gathered at Father Mehl's, this time amidst tumults of joy. Cardboard boxes, paper bundles, rucksacks, and old crates reveal their forbidden uniforms. They press the newly arrived Storm numbers onto their collar patches.

"Now that's something!"

"Let me see."

"Very posh!"

"Like a general on inspection."

"Now we finally look like proper subversives!"

Eventually they make such a racket that Schulz takes a worried look out of the window. There aren't just Nazis living here.

But circumstances require them to dress down a little.

They tuck the brown shirt collars under their suspenders, leaving their necks bare. Boots, brown trousers, caps, and belts are stored away. Extremely bourgeois trouser legs mingled with rough boots, strange waistcoats and jackets appear over their shirts.

And then the hats!

Looking at his horde, Schulz laughs so hard he almost suffocates.

There are blue peaked caps and boaters, Panama hats from the Thirty Years' War, stiff, dusty and dented bowlers, green Tyroleans with huge feathers, and even flamboyant Calabrians—a gruesome sight.

In awe of these grotesque disguises, they wave their military satchels.

"Well," says Schulz gloomily, "we won't get any further than the hallway. After the front door we are all getting arrested. That's how pretty we look."

And once again he gives his horde their final instructions, just in case. You never know.

"If someone's curious, you want to buy a plot of land in Machnow, understood? In the new Klein-Machnow settlement, got it?

They got it. They squeeze Father Mehl's hand, and then they're off. Well-mannered, well-behaved, two by two.

The wild crowd meets in Machnow. Suspicious-looking lads flock together from all sides.

Of course, the local policeman couldn't help but notice this suspicious crowd hanging around his district. But he can't quite figure out what's happening. Is this perhaps some kind of convention? Or a tramp meeting? In his district of all places?

And the more he looks around, the more he thinks that these guys don't really look like tramps. He knows tramps. These people here have different faces.

As the policeman is indecisively patrolling the area, he is startled by sudden shouting. A sharp voice cuts through the evening: "Fall in! Groups of four! Within the groups... right turn... march!"

In an instant, the wild bunch of suspicious lads has turned into a well-ordered, well-behaved troop, and now the policeman understands.

That's the Berlin SA!

His military eye estimates the troop to contain at least seven hundred men. Should he take action against this troop, which equates to almost half a regiment? Him alone?

No, he's not going to stop them. But there is a telephone. And he races towards it.

As the riot squad sirens are ringing through Machnow, the train is already whistling in the station, the engines are starting up, and the train starts to move. As the police cars arrive, their large headlights just barely illuminate a pretty sight: hundreds of waving SA hands, followed by the red tail lights of the train.

* * *

Slowly the train creeps into the Nuremberg station. And then a brown crowd floods the entire platform.

As they pass the barrier, Ede gives Schulz a hefty nudge. Ede has discovered something. Outside the station there is a huge crowd of people.

Ede whistles softly through his teeth. "Thick air outside," he says, "where they're standing!"

Schulz automatically reaches for the belt buckle and loosens his shoulder strap, and in this the whole Storm follows him. The Berlin SA has grown used to this rule of thumb: if a crowd of people gathers, they do so to fight the SA.

"So we don't get soft!" Schulz growls sarcastically as the Storm forms up. Then they leave through the station exit, confidently awaiting the first shouts and jostles.

And indeed, a thunderous roar rages against the tight-lipped SA-Men. But right away, their determination changes to utter astonishment... For this thundering roar is nothing more than a single, jubilant scream:

"Heil Hitler!"

"Heil Berlin!"

Completely bewildered and a little embarrassed, the Berliners stop where they are. Are they dreaming, or is this actually happening? Can there be such a thing? An assembly of a hundred thousand people shouting "Heil Hitler?" At first they peer suspiciously into the turmoil, but then their features soften, and they start to relax. Their fury and rage abate, their determination and willingness to fight, all of this is now dissolving and changing into an unbelievably powerful joy.

All seven hundred men of the Berlin SA start roaring in return, shouting, screaming, waving, and greeting. Not much would have been missing for the Berlin SA to start howling like overjoyed lapdogs.

And the surprises just keep coming. Now flowers are flying too!

Flowers over the SA! No, this can't be right.

But it is true.

It is exactly right.

Now a car slowly drives through the crowd and suddenly every member of the Berlin SA feels that burning flame again, spreading inside them from head to toe.

The Führer!

The Führer has come to the station to pick up his Berlin SA!

Like madmen, the SA rushes about, forming two arrays. The Führer slowly drives along their front, slowly, very slowly, from one man to the next, and he looks each one in the eye, every single one of them, and everyone returns his calm, serious look. You are the Führer; we are yours. Do with us what you want... what you want...

And then Berlin marches into their quarters, accompanied by cheering crowds.

"You really feel like you're on holiday," Schulz stutters, and Ede nods with emotion. "You know," he says, "it was just like this when we arrived in Riga!"[31]

Covered with flowers by the crowd, they fix those flowers on their belts, their chests and caps. Now and then they hear shouts from within the crowd, and these shouts fill them with pride. "The Berliners!" the people of Nuremberg shout to each other. "The Berliners!!!"

Schulz turns around to his boys. "Let's get home soon," he shouts, "Berlin needs to become just like this!"

"On our honor!" they yell back.

---

[31] The German Army entered Riga in 1917 in the last major military operation in the East during the First World War. Riga was heavily populated by ethnic Baltic Germans, who would greet them as liberators.

The Führer and Dr. Goebbels at the 1929 Nuremberg Party Convention.

17

MISFORTUNE

But that's not how it is in Berlin yet. On the contrary, quite the opposite!

Dog-tired and overjoyed, the Berlin SA drives back home. The night before Monday they return by train, sleeping in the railway carriages. They sleep in the luggage nets and on the floor, on the benches and anywhere else where a human body can find the place to lie down. They are in for a sudden awakening, as signals sound and doors are ripped open. Those closest to the doors receive blows with rifle butts to the ribs.

What the hell is going on?

They'll know soon.

The deputy police commissioner receives the SA at the city borders of the Reich capital.

Oh, Isidor! the SA thinks grimly.

"Everyone out!!!"

The sleepy SA-Men slowly get out of the train. In the early dawn light they can see trucks waiting for them.

"Time to get coffee!" Schulz shouts cheerfully, but a blow to the back of his knees turns him quiet.

They are driven onto the trucks with rubber truncheons. Smoking and singing are forbidden. Same goes for whistling, shouting, and lying down.

The entire Berlin SA has been arrested. They are taken where criminals are usually taken to, Alexanderplatz. The investigation is already on the way. Mr. Weiss knows that the Berlin SA has been awarded two flags by the Führer. And Isidor wants these flags at all costs.

The officers begin their search. In a feverish haste, the standard-bearer has cut cloth from shaft, hiding it under his shirt. But it is already too late. The officers have watched him, and now eight of them grab the standard-bearer and tear off his shirt. Tears of anger run down his cheeks. He doesn't make it easy for the police.

Until blows from rubber truncheons bring about his collapse.

An hour later a song rises from the convoy, from all the cars and all the lips. The eternal, holy song dashes through a still half-slumbering Berlin. Under carbine blows and rubber truncheons, they sing, handcuffed, with battered faces and torn shirts, seven hundred arrested SA-Men sing: "Deutschland, Deutschland über alles!"[32]

No threats can mute them. No cudgel can silence them.

Berlin stops, listens, and freezes.

What? Didn't they report that the NSDAP was finished? Dead and done for? Didn't they read that the SA had been banned?

But there they are, driving car after car, the finished, dead, forbidden SA!

There they go, "...und im Unglück nun erst recht!"[33]

*   *   *

The interrogations are very long, precise, and thorough. Again and again, they rummage through the SA's possessions.

Uniforms are confiscated, trousers, shirts, and caps.

On Monday evening they start to release them one by one. And the Commune, which has joyfully gathered on Alexanderplatz, rushes to attack these individuals. The last one to leave police headquarters is Storm Leader Daluege. He stayed until he knew for sure that none of his SA-Men were still left in the building.

When those SA-Men with a job appear at their workplaces on Tuesday morning, they find their position already occupied.

"Absenteeism without excuse. Sorry, there are enough workers in Berlin."

That day, Berlin would gain a few hundred more unemployed people.

---

[32] "Germany, Germany above all" is the opening verse of the German national anthem, "Das Deutschlandlied" or "The Song of the Germans." After 1945, its first two stanzas are no longer part of the German national anthem and their use is stigmatized in popular society. Only the third stanza ("Unity and Justice and Freedom...") remains in use today.
[33] "...and in misfortune more than ever" is part of a later addition to "The Song of the Germans" by Albert Matthai. This fourth stanza, also known as a "spite stanza," was added in 1921 as a reaction to the lost war and the Versailles treaty, but never officially became part of the national anthem.

Astonishingly, the press reports that the Berlin SA had been arrested for assaulting young workers in Erlangen.

The SA is confused. Young workers? In Erlangen?

They did not even arrive via Erlangen!—But apparently that doesn't matter to the press.

18

CELEBRATION

All this being said, one cannot deny that they have gained some momentum.

Schulz notices it because he sells more newspapers than before. *The Attack* goes quite well. As it turns out, mass arrest of the Berlin SA made for a great NSDAP advertisement. Completely free of charge!

Gauleiter Dr. Goebbels is served with a renewed ban on speaking.

Next to a large official stamp, the document contains the following signature:

P.P.
Krause
Chancellery Assistant.

The next evening Schulz reads Dr. Goebbels' reply from *The Attack* to his boys.

"I, Krause, will therefore strike the Constitution's cheek, deny Dr. Goebbels the freedom of expression guaranteed to every German, and if he should dare to speak out anyway, will proceed to dissolve the assembly. Bad Krause! Trembling, we witness your terrible threats. Before each meeting, we shall not fail to pose this shy question: 'Is Krause in the house?'"

The SA roars with laughter, and all of a sudden they have a new song for their way home. Consisting of only four verses and a terrible melody, it goes like this:

"Is Krause, is Krause...
In the house... in the house?
No, he's not here...
But we are..."

And then they mumble something else, which almost seems like some kind of fifth verse. One can't quite understand it, but it sounds kind of like: *...the SA... the SA...*

But of course this cannot be, because the SA has been banned.

Oh, but however bold and daring *The Attack* may seem night after night, it is not doing well.

That damn lack of money!

It is simply unbelievable how much money it takes to run a newspaper!

What's more, Dr. Goebbels will have to pay back the two thousand marks he borrowed quite soon. Bankruptcy vultures already lift their wings, letting their embarrassing calls ring out!

The Doctor does not speak a word about it.

But the SA knows about it. They know that he is plagued by worries. They also know that the Gauleiter is being dragged to court on an almost daily basis, that they're trying to wear him down with endless negotiations of ridiculous and foolish trifles.

And still he is forbidden to talk.

The old fighters are having a meeting, Daluege, Geyer and others. Schulz happens to be there as well. "Even the strongest man couldn't stand that in the long run," mumbles Schulz, "always without the slightest bit of joy, always trouble, courts, harassment from all sides. And then the worries start..."

They are talking about the Doctor. And they agree that something must be done. And when they part that evening, they are clear about what it is they're going to do.

Daluege is delighted. For the first time ever, they are going to deceive the Doctor about something, all of them together. And they're going to do it in a very systematic way. It will be damn hard, but they will keep silent. And the Doctor has not the slightest clue. He writes his razor-sharp essays in *The Attack* and gives his orders for the various sports, savings, beer, gymnastics, and other clubs that they've been founding; he stands in court again and again and he works for the party.

Slowly, far too slowly for his horde of deceivers, the 29th of October comes around.

The 29th of October is the birthday of Dr. Joseph Goebbels.

At first, the day doesn't seem particularly special. His employees recite their congratulations, closing with a resounding "Heil Hitler!" shake hands with him and are quite pleased with the extraordinarily fitting birthday present that the Doctor received from police headquarters.

Today of all days, Dr. Goebbels is allowed to talk again. Nobody knows why it came and why it arrived on his birthday, but it's certainly a very nice way of celebrating a birthday.

As evening approaches, two of the old fighters pick up the Doctor from his flat. They don't tell him where they're going. They just tell him to come along; he might even enjoy it.

The Doctor good-naturedly goes with them. They walk through many streets until they enter a restaurant with a big hall, and when the surprised Doctor curiously peeks through the door, he sees the entire SA and many, many party comrades. And like a single unit everyone rises and yells "Hail!" and "Congratulations!" and "Long may he live!" A giant uproar.

Whether he wants to or not, he has to get up on the grandstand, and then Schulz joins him for a little speech. He hands him a very pretty muzzle, referring to it as a "legally trademarked Isidor mask."

At the sight of their Gauleiter speechlessly holding his muzzle, the hall erupts in roars of laughter.

And already the next congratulant is standing next to him.

He delivers a large package for the Doctor to open. Inside he finds a cardboard box, and in that cardboard box there are two thousand five hundred new *The Attack* subscriptions. Schulz and his men have collected them feverishly in the weeks before.

There stands Dr. Goebbels, who has just been allowed to speak again by the police commissioner, but not a single word makes it past his lips.

Now the tall Daluege appears, waving an envelope in his hands, and this envelope contains two thousand marks. Two thousand marks cash, so the publisher of *The Attack* can finally get rid of his urgent debts. Two thousand marks, collected by party comrades! And last but not least there is a second envelope. When the Doctor tears it open, he finds the torn debt certificate for the two thousand marks he borrowed.

And before the utterly surprised man, who on his thirtieth birthday receives such strange gifts, only one of which, a muzzle, goes to himself while all the others go to the party... before he can even begin to utter his thanks, Schulz swings himself onto a table and reads out the joint congratulations of the Berlin SA to their Doctor.

And their congratulations go like this:

Lieba Dokta!

*Wir Balina brauchen eenen, der uffmeebelt, wissen Se, so mit
Schwunk und Jrazie. Weil wir det wissen, det Sie wat keen, un
wenn denn so eener von die Brider kommt und Ihnen mit dolle
Sachen und Jemeinheiten anspucken tut, lassense man, davor
haben wa Ihnen jerne. Also, hochzuvaehrenda Dokta, wehrta
Volksjenosse, wir jratulieren also wie jesacht und winschen Sie
allet Jute vor die Kämpferei, wat uns jar nich doll jenuch
herjehen kann und ibahaupt mit Sie, wo allet mitmacht.*

Dear Doctor!

*Us Berliners need someone who gets things going, you know,
with some dash and style. And because we know that you get
things done, don't worry about those guys who try to accuse and
insult you. We'll always like you. So, most revered Doctor, dear
Comrade, like I already said, we congratulate you and wish you
all the best for the fights to come. You know how we like to get
rough, especially with someone like you who is always game for
anything.* [34]

Yes, that's the Berlin SA.

Dr. Joseph Goebbels may have had trouble going to sleep that
night. With men such as these, Berlin will be conquered. Slowly they
are making progress.

The following spring, on May 20th, twelve National Socialists
move into the German Reichstag.

---

[34] The literal translation cannot do justice to the brilliant Berlin vernacular. Instead,
imagine a half-drunk, half-disgruntled but deeply affectionate middle-aged man with an
inability to pronounce the letter "g" reading these words.

19

VACATION

But before that Schulz is in for a rare experience. He goes on vacation, a real actual holiday. For an entire Sunday.

That works out quite well, because at the moment there is no top cellar to look after, no communist printing press to disrupt, and no duty scheduled in the Storm.

He doesn't have to think long about what he wants to do with this free Sunday. He would like to go to the Mark again, to those small, neat Mark villages; he has discovered his homeland. And so, come Sunday morning, he leaves with Hermann, a few sandwiches, and a pitcher of cold coffee.

"It's the only right thing to do," he explains to Hermann at length, "in the old days, all we did was go into town, without a clue about the outside world, about a homeland and all that. Sometimes to Treptow, sometimes to Spandau, and sometimes even Tegel—that was all we did. Until all of a sudden you find out that there is such a thing as the countryside, you know, actual countryside with goats and chickens and church bells. I wrote down all the place I still have to go. Here, take a look."

He spreads out a large piece of paper.

As the train starts to roll, the Heath flies by, the pines, fields, and meadows.

Hermann studies the paper which Schulz has filled with all the names of villages and towns he wants to visit, one after another. As an old Wandervögel, Hermann cannot help but giggle. Schulz seems to have drafted a ten-year plan.

"So now I'll be going to all of those places, a different town each quarter. Can't really do it more frequently, you know? Won't have enough cash, and then there's SA duty..."

Hermann nods in amazement.

None of this is new for Hermann. As a Wandervogel he has been roaming the Mark plenty. At ten years old he had already been pretty much everywhere. It is hard for him to imagine that there are Berliners who have no idea about the Mark and have to experience this beautiful, powerful, and dreamy landscape like a miracle, a revelation.

Curious and a little anxious, he looks at the list Schulz is holding out to him. There they are, all neatly written down, the Mark's crown jewels: Schwedt an der Oder and Vierraden, Belzig and Wiesenburg, Rathenow, Wittenberge, Gransee, Lychen, Prenzlau, Rheinsberg, Friesack Castle, Joachimsthal, Chorin, Boitzenburg, Alt-Landsberg, Stendal and Küstrin and so on and so on.

Home, thinks Hermann, as he reads this. Can there be such a thing, home on a piece of paper?

Longing for a homeland—he begins to understand, and he is almost ashamed of the fact that he experienced all of this and almost took it for granted, never even thinking much about it. That at best he noticed the sheer beauty of the Mark Brandenburg, with its heath and sands, the lakes and forests, its old towns with their towers and defiant buildings. And suddenly he realizes that this man next to him, SA-Man Schulz, may have seen half the world during the Great War. But the world he fought for, the things for which he put his head on the line... he is only just discovering them. And it is only through Adolf Hitler that he started to discover them. The blood rushes to the boy's head.

And as the train approaches Prenzlau, Hermann takes Schulz by the hand and says, half pleading, half comforting: "Let's take more of these trips together. Yes?"

Schulz glances at him, when suddenly he realizes that this lad, who is still half a child, has been thinking about him, about the movement and about their homeland. And he responds: "Yes, and then maybe we'll get to see where we actually come from."

He says "we," but it is clear that he really means, "where I come from."

"Now that would be interesting."

Then both of them look out the window for a long time.

Because it is incredibly hard to talk about such things. Then Hermann remembers a song, which he heard and sang a long time ago. Their conversation has stirred up his memory and now he understands it quite differently, more deeply, more fully. It is no longer just an ordinary song, like so many thousands of others. Now it has become a confession, a beautiful, enticing hymn. As the train pulls into the station, Hermann fervently sings the song, and Schulz listens attentively:

Märkische Heide, märkischer Sand,
Sind des Märkers Freude, sind sein Heimatland.
Steige hoch, du roter Adler,
Hoch über Sumpf und Sand,
Hoch über dunkle Kiefernwälder,
Heil dir, mein Brandenburger Land,
Hoch über dunkle Kiefernwälder,
Heil dir, mein Brandenburger Land.[35]

Markish heath, Markish sand,
Our joy is this homeland,
Rise up high, red eagle,
High above swamp and sand,
High above dark pinewoods,
Hail, my Brandenburgian land,
High above dark pinewoods,
Hail, my Brandenburgian land.

---

[35] The title of this song is "Brandenburglied," also known as "Märkische Heide," or "Märkish Heath"

20

SIEGE

As they leave the Pasewalk station, Schulz suddenly stops.

"Damn it, Hermann," he says, "there's trouble!"

"Why?" asks Hermann in amazement. He can see and hear absolutely nothing that even remotely resembles trouble.

"Dunno," says Schulz, "old warrior, sixth sense and all that. I can smell a brawl in the air. Guess we're lucky we look like civilians today."

And as they start to wander through the town, even Herman notices that there is indeed something strange going on. They meet some very familiar-looking faces, which remind them strikingly of Red Front men.

"Aha," growls Schulz, "well, let's go on a little patrol."

Eagerly they march off. All of a sudden neither the fields nor the town hall are of any interest. And ten minutes later the case is solved. Schulz whistles through his teeth as they arrive at the Schützenhaus.[36] Because this Pasewalker Schützenhaus is occupied by Berlin's Storm 1, in front of the Schützenhaus lurks the Commune. But lo and behold, between the parties they can see Landjägers.[37]

"The sausage lads!" whispers Schulz.

"Of course!" Hermann whispers back.

Well, well, thinks Schulz, *so that's how it works in Pasewalk: The Commune and the Landjägers jointly besieging a Nazi Storm.*

And together with Hermann, he inches a little closer. Suddenly there's an uproar as the Landjägers and Communists launch a little

---

[36] A Schützenhaus is a type of building that can be found in various German towns and cities. Essentially, they are shooting ranges operated and maintained by dedicated shooting clubs (formerly guilds). Often they also include small bars or pubs for club members and visitors.

[37] Previously the Royal Prussian State Gendarmerie, renamed in 1920. "Landjäger" also refers to a type of dried sausage, still popular throughout Germany.

assault on the Schützenhaus. But its doors and windows are tightly barricaded. They can't get Storm 1 out.

"They won't leave that spot anytime soon," Schulz remarks quietly, "And to get them out, they'll need howitzers, bombs, and flamethrowers. And they don't seem to have brought any, thank God."

Then the two wander around the Schützenhaus, but things look just the same in the back. Here too, there are Landjägers and communists. A beer glass comes flying from the Schützenhaus, missing Schulz's head by a hair's breadth.

"Pity!" he yells in annoyance, meaning it is a pity that this beautiful glass did not land on a communist's head. The two of them retreat into cover, and Schulz wonders how they could intervene. Storm 1 needs help, dammit! Something must be done! Suddenly an absurd idea pops into his head, causing a slight giggle. But why not give it a try? He grabs Hermann by the arm and they disappear into the next inn. Inside, a cheeky Schulz piously asks to use the telephone.

He calls the Reichswehr, demanding the officer on duty.

"Excuse me?" a dumbfounded officer asks. "Landjägers and communists together? I don't quite think that's possible, my good man."

"Fine," replies Schulz, "then the place will go to pieces, and we'll have a civil war.

"Alright," says the officer at the other end hesitantly, "I'll call it in."

Schulz and Hermann walk back to the Schützenhaus. The siege is continuing. There they stand, surrounded by communists, and wait for the things to come. Maybe the Reichswehr Offizier has some backbone and will arrive with the guard. Maybe he's not even allowed to. Maybe... maybe...

At that moment a shutter opens on the second floor of the Schützenhaus and a volley of beer glasses comes flying. Right then Schulz gets another one of his stupid ideas. Completely indifferent about the glasses bursting everywhere around them, he looks straight towards the open window and then raises his right arm in greeting.

He quickly lowers it again.

The communists didn't notice anything. But Schulz hopes that their comrades in the Schützenhaus did.

"If they aren't completely retarded, they'll notice the two of us," he growls.

Hermann is dumbfounded by this daring undertaking.

A few minutes go by until Schulz can observe the slow opening of a ground floor shutter and again Schulz raises his right arm up, no longer caring about the Communist's reaction, no longer caring whether the whole mob will descend unto them. The two of them stare intently at the house.

And now the downstairs door actually opens.

Schulz yells "Go!" and the two of them chase towards the house with long strides. Before the stunned communists realize what's going on, they have disappeared through the front door.

The door is slammed shut and locked again. Schulz and Hermann are still breathing heavily from their frantic run.

In the corridor's twilight a young man stands before them, probably even younger than Hermann. "My name is Horst Wessel, Storm 1," he says.

"Pleased to meetcha," Schulz grumbles happily, "I'm Schulz, and this is Hermann..."

"I will go make my report to the Sturmführer," a calm Wessel interrupts him and leaves.

There is little talk between them, because the chaos outside has started up again.

It's a veritable shoot-out in front of the Schützenhaus.

"I have called the Reichswehr," Schulz reports hesitantly. The Sturmführer nods.

"I did that as well. The phone in here still works."

Well then. So my idea wasn't stupid after all, a satisfied Schulz thinks to himself. Then he and Hermann go searching for the young man who received them down in the hallway.

His name was Horst Wessel, and this young person made quite an impression on Schulz. He doesn't quite know why, since they only spoke for a few seconds. But still...

* * *

Thirty minutes later the Reichswehr arrives. They do not take kindly to the Communists; they are in fact quite rude. They are not particularly polite towards the Landjägers either.

Then they knock at the Schützenhaus gate.

Storm 1 surrenders to the Reichswehr.

Accompanied by columns of soldiers to the left and right, Storm 1 marches towards the train station.

As the train starts rolling, the Reichswehr officer slowly raises a hand to his helmet. His salute continues until the last car has disappeared from the platform.

By some fateful circumstance, Hermann, Schulz, and Wessel have ended up in the same compartment. As the train rattles homewards, they are engaged in a lively conversation.

What are they talking about?

Well about the SA of course, about their marches, the Führer, and Dr. Goebbels.

What else would these SA-Men be talking about?

They exchange many of their numerous memories. Schulz for example recounts the first SA march through red Neukölln.

The young SA-Man by the name of Horst Wessel listens devoutly, although sometimes it seems as if he wants to interrupt the older man, to confirm his explanations or to ask a question. The story seems to excite him to the utmost.

Schulz recalls, "That was almost nothing today, and if it weren't for those stupid Landjägers, we would have cleaned up the Commune, finished them off, and made it back home for dinner by now. But you should have been there on November 26th, when Gener gave his stupid order to take a walk through Rixdorf... Well actually it wasn't that stupid, he was absolutely right, and it was a great provocation. I still remember it like it was yesterday. Really, it was actually the beginning of all this.

"So, on November 11th we go for a meeting at the Kaiser-Friedrich-Straße station. Already a catastrophe. Imagine, you're in full uniform and have to come alone to that station! Well, and so it went. The first guys who arrived all had to get their heads bandaged, every single one of them. But at least they were there. Then more and more arrive until finally we were about three hundred men. Communists all around us, staring at us, trying to figure out which one of us they were going to tear into pieces first. They didn't start tearing right away, but that wasn't too surprising. We know those guys; they like to have a little fun first. Well, and then we started! *Fall in! Attention! In formations*"—and so on."

"And then?" Wessel interjects impatiently.

"No cops?" asks Hermann.

"Yes and no," Schulz continues, "first nothing happened, I mean nothing at all happened, you know. Of course there wasn't any police. They were a little too fond of their health, and who can blame them for that? Police patrols through Neukölln are still more like a suicide squad, even today.

"So we start to drum up a storm, the Commune starts shouting all around us, and we march off into the thick of it. And from street to street, things are getting trickier. The cute communist broads are screaming like crazy from all the windows. The street starts to narrow from all the people to the left and right. Well, now it's probably going to start. You couldn't even hear our drums anymore. At this point all we could march to were the ups and downs of communist shouts. They still had a rhythm, so we marched to that, and in pretty good order.

"And you know, the singing... that was a whole other thing. Pretty meager. We didn't have any real songs, nothing that could compete with the Internationale. We just didn't have any and so–"

"That's it!" Horst Wessel interrupts him excitedly, "that's exactly it! I thought about that so often! There you are, marching along, everyone is doing well, things look quite good, you feel like you're winning... and all of a sudden they start singing: *'The Internationale unites the human race.'* There is something to this song, you can bet on that. It's not a bad song, it comes with a spark and there is something in the melody that carries you away—*'this is the final struggle!'*—Yes, yes!"

"Now, now!" Hermann tries to pacify him, but Wessel angrily rejects this.

"Good Lord, everyone knows that! There's a big gathering. Neat. You talk and talk and talk and you're on a roll. Then a red speaker walks up to the podium and tries to debate, producing nothing but a bunch of crap. Now you're looking forward to annihilating this gentleman in your closing statement, and then all of a sudden they start singing: *'So comrades, come rally! And the last fight let us face!'* And then a thousand men are singing your ears off. A thousand men who have just forgotten everything that you've been painstakingly laying out for them. They may have been partially agreeing with you already! But whenever they hear this song, they are bewitched. Doesn't matter how much you've talked—as soon as someone starts singing the song, it was in vain; you might as well have talked to the wall. I know because I've seen it before: whole assemblies in vain, just because the Internationale has such colossal power. Don't you understand that?"

"Sure," Hermann hesitantly admits, "but we have songs as well man!"

"Songs! Songs!" Wessel continues, "of course we have songs! A whole lot of them! But I want to tell you something: we don't have that one song! Yes, that one big song to push the Internationale against the wall. We need to have our own Internationale, and of course it would be called Nationale, because that's what we're missing."

"But we have the Deutschlandlied for that," remarks Hermann thoughtfully.

Wessel notices that they don't quite get his meaning yet. But now he's getting fired up, because the time has come to get a problem off his chest which he's been thinking about for a long time. The whole compartment is listening. People are joining them from nearby compartments until finally he's surrounded by a devout audience.

"The Deutschlandlied," he explains, "the Deutschlandlied is meant for celebrations, you see? But it is not meant for gatherings like ours, right on the cusp of turning into a brawl! Worthless! With the Deutschlandlied you can never go up against the Internationale. And our SA Song: *Freedom is not lost as long as a heart desires it*—it's wonderful, but much too slow. And what else do we have—maybe: *'Swastika on a steel helmet?'* What do you mean, steel helmet? We need a song that includes all of us, something for everyone and not just veterans of the blessed Kapp-Putsch!"[38]

The compartment has become quiet.

Then Schulz slowly responds, "Well, you're not wrong. But we don't have one and we can't just make one. When the time comes, we'll have that song, don't worry about it. Something like that just happens. You can't just write something like that. And now let's go on with the story. As we arrive at Hermannplatz, our standard-bearer starts to feel a little queasy and he gently begins to roll up the flag. Little by little, you know. At first we thought it was just the wind, rolling up the flag bit by bit. Eventually it got too much though and the troop leader went up to the boy to give him a piece of his mind—suddenly it fluttered nicely again.

"And then the cops came and sealed off our march from all spectators. And that's how we got through unhurt. The Commune was bursting with rage, I can tell you that much. Later on we did a little housecleaning with our commando squads, but that march really was

---

[38] The Kapp-Putsch was an attempted coup by right-wing autocratic elements within the Reichswehr and the newly organized Freikorps. Named after one of its key instigators, Wolfgang Kapp, the coup lasted only around four days, from March 13th to March 17th, 1920, before being foiled by a general strike, which rendered much of the basic infrastructure such as postal service, public transit, and in some cases even water and electricity unusable to the newly self-appointed rulers.

the best part.

"But when we eventually parted at Hallesches Tor to go back home one by one, they stormed our tram wagons. That wasn't so nice. That was one of those real, cowardly Commune moves. During our march, no one dared to come close. But when we were on our own, we suddenly had thirty people injured."

Schulz has finished his story. For a while, they sit in complete silence. Every one of them has had experiences that were just like that or at least extremely similar. It was not by coincidence that their faces have turned hard and unyielding since they joined the SA.

Then the train arrives in Berlin. They roll by the desolate rear buildings, blackened by smoke, and this sight doesn't exactly improve their mood. Wessel points to those derelict walls. Their plaster is eroding, falling down bit by bit. Their windows are blind and unseeing, except for the occasional pale face of a child.

"We must have those people," Wessel announces into the silence, "the people living in those houses, we must get them. They have lost all hope in life. We must return that hope to them. We have to get those workers; we have to get them…"

The others just nod in silent agreement. Then they leave the train and disperse in front of Stettin station. Horst Wessel, Schulz, and Hermann.

21

ANTHEM

There comes the day when Standard[39] 4 marches in front of the Karl Liebknecht House.

In front of that very house where the heart of German communism beats fanatically and unceasingly. These walls house the most destructive idea ever to descend on the world. Inside these headquarters, unscrupulous people work on bringing Bolshevism to Europe. They work day and night, using any means necessary.

If the world press had understood what was going on that day and the importance of that march, it would have mobilized hundreds of its best reporters to accompany Standard 4 on their march. For as the unknown European vanguard was about to take on the blood-red star of Lenin, the lost German youth prepared for their storm. Standard 4 marched in a solemn demonstration against the subverters of their most sacred beliefs.

If the world press had understood the immense danger Bolshevism posed to Europe and the world, it would not have limited itself to delivering witty and thought-provoking reports from Soviet Russia that day. If it had noticed the stench of decay emanating from the East, it would have told of the six hundred SA-Men marching against the KPD, covered it with huge headlines and column-length reports.

But the world press did not possess such basic instincts. They failed to understand that on this very day a handful of determined men were defending an ancient culture, that they were issuing a serious warning against the criminals who laid out their mines and

---

[39] *Standarten* ("Standards") were organizational units used to structure the SA. Each *Standarte* consisted of three to five *Sturmbanne* ("Storm Groups," roughly equivalent to a battalion), and each *Sturmbann* consisted of three to five *Stürme* ("Storms," roughly equivalent to companies). Every *Sturm* contained three to four *Truppen*, ("Troops," roughly equivalent to platoons).

booby traps in the very heart of this culture.

Standard 4 does not carry any weapons other than their serious and determined faces. They are well aware of the fateful route their march will take them on: the Karl Liebknecht House is located on Bülowplatz,[40] right in the center of North Berlin.

Before they set out on this march, the Standard leader speaks a few words to them: "The communists will try to disturb us. In contrast, the SA maintains iron discipline. We will maintain close formation throughout our march, under any and all circumstances.

"When we are attacked—remain in close formation! And now— raise our flag!—Standard 4—march!"

In Storm 1, a young SA-Man startles violently. What did the Standard leader just say?

"Remain in close formation—raise our flag–"

SA-Man Horst Wessel feels as if he was just hit by lightning. *These words are like a song!—a song!—a song,* he thinks, mechanically marching along, almost in a frenzy—remain in close formation—raise our flag—that's how the song should sound and then—our brown battalions—hope and confidence... Go ahead, shout "Down!" all you want, keep covering your Liebknecht House with endless banners, put up your Soviet flag everywhere you want—soon all of us will carry Hitler's flag—yes, that's just how the song should be...

An intoxicated Horst Wessel returns home. His hands are dry and hot, his head glowing.

He hardly speaks a word to anyone; he just sits there brooding. Just around midnight, his brother and sister are roused from sleep. What in God's name has gone into Horst? Singing and playing the piano in the middle of the night! They climb out of their beds to listen for a bit. They walk up to him. He just keeps on singing. They look over his rumpled head, trying to decipher the lyrics on his almost illegible music sheet. It doesn't take long before they can sing along.

They are singing a brand-new song, which feels strangely familiar at the same time. It is a provocative battle hymn, while also reminding them of an ancient folk song.

In the dead of night, three young people are singing:

---

[40] After undergoing a series of name changes throughout the events of these years and the decades that followed, the square is now called Rosa-Luxemburg-Platz.

Raise our flag, remain in close formation,
SA march on with calm and steady stride!
Comrades killed by Red Front and Reaction's ruination,
Today they march in spirit side by side!

Clear all the street for our brown battalions!
Clear all the street for storm commando men!
These hopeful eyes, the swastika guides millions,
This new dawn makes them full and free again.

At last we hear this final call to action,
Every last man stands ready for this fight,
Soon Hitler's flag is carried by each faction,
It won't be long until we regain our right!

Raise our flag, remain in close formation,
SA march on with calm and steady stride!
Comrades killed by Red Front and Reaction's ruination,
Today they march in spirit side by side!

* * *

Ten months later, the Berlin Gauleiter writes: "Already browns throughout the country are singing this song. In ten years' time children will sing it, workers in their factories, soldiers on the streets! I can already see columns marching, these endless columns, endless, endless. A humiliated people rises and sets itself in motion. It resounds from millions of throats, the song of the German Revolution: 'Raise our Flag.'"[41]

It would not take ten years for the song to be sung by all of Germany.

---

[41] Horst Wessel's song, which became known as "Horst-Wessel-Lied" and also by it's opening words "Die Fahne hoch" ("Raise our Flag"), became the anthem of the NSDAP from 1930–1945 and co-national anthem of Germany, along with the first stanza of the "Deutschlandlied," from 1933–1945. After WWII, the song was subsequently banned.

22

Undercover

Four times Horst Wessel gets offered the post of Sturmführer, three times a position as Reichsredner, and finally the rank of Oberführer in Mecklenburg.

When Schulz meets him once again, Horst Wessel has chosen the post of squad leader. Squad 34, Friedrichshain.

And that is a suicide commando.

But Horst Wessel has turned a lost and neglected Squad 34 into Storm 5, the most famous Storm of Berlin.

Seeing him, Schulz cannot help but grin. "They say that trouble is extremely beneficial to one's health... take care of yourself, son."

"Take care?" laughs Wessel, "well, maybe sometimes. You wanna come along with me tonight? I'm about to go somewhere."

"Of course," a curious Schulz replies. They walk off together.

Wessel is heading for a really shady area. As they walk along, he shares some solid advice with Schulz.

"If for whatsoever reason you cannot help but cry out *'Heil Hitler'* tonight, please make sure you call a hearse first."

Then they arrive at Mexico Pub.

The Mexico Pub is a pub with character. Even in its namesake country it would definitely have to be considered... interesting. Greasy whores with pale faces and thickly applied make-up, their voices shrill from drinking are lolling around the tables. Young, pink-eyed men are sitting next to them with flushed cheeks and slovenly expressions. A cheap music box supplies some horrible background noise.

An old drunk in a dirty suit and a blue cap sits at the bar, telling dirty stories to two young boys.

To the left sits a platinum blonde woman, about thirty years of age. From there she directs three young girls who keep hurrying back and forth throughout the pub.

An impenetrable cloud of cigar smoke hovers around the place. Wessel and Schulz have to pause a few seconds to catch their breath before planting themselves down at a table next to the door.

For a brief moment, they receive some indifferent looks from the other guests.

Wessel leans a little towards Schulz.

"This is where the Commune does politics," he mumbles, "police will never enter here. The blonde over there is the leader of the Red Women's and Girls' Federation. Fine people in here, huh? And those three over at the bar, the blue cap with the two boys, you'd bet they're cooking up a burglary, right? But they're doing something entirely different: they're cooking up their next assault on the SA. More specifically, my SA, Storm 5."

Schulz feels the goosebumps running over his skin. Sitting here is beyond impudent—it's an audacity of the first order. The thought makes him grin.

"Unbelievable!" he growls appreciatively, "You're really something!"

"Small expedition into the enemy trench," Wessel whispers back, "I can understand that you probably don't like this place very much. But I have to keep looking at this milieu, you know, again and again. So I can tell the German worker what these communist ladies and gentlemen look like, what they are like. So he can see who has the presumption to play his leaders. And so he knows to whom he is entrusting his sons and daughters."

On their way home, Schulz pensively asks: "Tell me, Wessel, what did you do before this? You got a job or not?"

Wessel smiles. "What I did? I would rather tell you what I am. Student, corps student, worker, and SA-Man. Because you can be all of those things at the same time. They do not detract from each other."

Schulz is amazed.

"My father was a pastor," Wessel says, before changing the topic. "And now let me sing you our new Storm Song."

They have just arrived at Unter den Linden, but Wessel doesn't worry about that. Pulling Schulz along with him on this beautiful, broad avenue, he sings his song:

Ob Ausmarsch oder Versammlungsschlacht
Wir müssen es immer beweisen!
Ob vor uns die Schupopistole kracht,
Ob die Luft voller Steine und Eisen!
Ja in jedem Falle geht Mann für Mann
Vom fünften Sturm an den Feind heran...[42]

March, Assembly, Brawl or Battle,
We always have to prove it!
Whether a policeman's pistol cracks,
Or the air is full of iron and stones!
We still do not mind to get close,
As the fifth Storm pursues its foes!

Then Sturmführer Horst Wessel and SA-Man Schulz separate. One of them trots off towards Father Mehl's place, the other towards Jüdenstraße. They would never see each other again.

Communist threat against Standard
Leader Knüppel at his Berlin residence

---

[42] The song Bade's Horst Wessel sings is a rather obscure one. The only other mention of it appears in a youth movement pamphlet dedicated to Horst Wessel, in which the lyrics are labeled as a "poem by Horst Wessel." As this pamphlet was dated 1939, six years after the publishing of Conquering Berlin in 1933, it is possible that Bade's book served as the initial source. Bade in turn may have simply invented it himself to flesh out his Horst Wessel character a little further.

Horst Wessel as Leader of Storm 5.

23

Debate

Shortly before the party conference in 1929 Horst Wessel had a memorable conversation with Doctor of Philosophy Hans Gerkenrath, Germanist and expert on medieval art. This conversation took place at the corner of Friedrichstraße and Unter den Linden and lasted one and a half hours.

Dr. Gerkenrath did not mince his words and was not at all embarrassed to express his opinion. "You are most skilled," he said ironically, "at screwing up your future. Although I would have thought you were a little more imaginative in this respect. Jokes aside"—and Gerkenrath became serious—"what's the point of sitting around in stupid pubs and fighting with Marxists and altogether living like a stupid foot soldier? Man—think about it, can that be a life goal? After all, you are a corps student, an excellent lawyer, and could have a great career, if you only want to.

"And what do you do? You roam around Wedding, get yourself beaten bloody and beat others bloody in return. Man, Horst, if you want to see blood, just have a Mensur[43] and stab around according to customs, as it befits a person of your education. When I look at you, a cold rage overcomes me. You are also a very good writer and generally a talented guy. How you, as an intellectual person–"

Horst Wessel stops in his tracks and suddenly has a sharp wrinkle on his clean and clear forehead. "Hold it," he says, "just a moment. Now you have finally given me the cue. I'm aware that you won't understand a hint of what I'm about to tell you, so I might as well speak Chinese to you. But I want to speak Chinese with you for once. Here's the thing: I come from a pastor's house, I am well educated, have received my higher school certificate, belong to the Kösener SC.,

---

[43] The traditional German academic-fraternity duel fought with sharp swords.

Normannia, Alemannia, two excellent corps. I study law with pleasure and love. I write poems and novellas on the side. I love literature and I love music and so I am, as you so aptly said, an intellectual person. I also have quite good manners, don't I? I've never gobbled up fish with a knife, and I can kiss a lady's hand without that hand getting wet from my nose–"

Horst Wessel interrupted himself and smiled, because Gerkenrath had twisted his mouth painfully.

"Excuse me, Hans, I was just about to fall into my rough SA tone. For your sake I will try to continue speaking in a refined voice. Well, I am an intellectual person, we have established that. I have immersed myself in Goethe and I love romanticism, Schlegel, Tieck, Novalis. I idolize Hölderlin and know my Nietzsche and my Kant, and so I am an intellectual person. And I can tell and explain to you what the *dolus eventualis* is all about and what the law of the ancient Romans looked like in the time of one much honored Mr. Caesar.

"So I cannot repeat often enough that I am an intellectual man. And now listen carefully. I have put aside these spiritual possessions of mine for now. I live in dreadful shacks that smell of cabbage soup and barley coffee, as I mostly eat cabbage soup and drink barley coffee. And I fight in the streets as often as it has to be—and it has to be very often—with riled up German workers, with criminals and pimps. I have a brown shirt and I march with my comrades, and these comrades of mine are 'simple workers,' as you would condescendingly call these German people, who may well be the best of us. I sit around in my Storm pubs. I serve twenty-four hours a day in the SA, and I don't earn a penny."

"Well, yes," Gerkenrath offered most reluctantly, but Wessel didn't let him speak.

"I am far from finished. So, I have put aside for now everything that is my spiritual possession. And now listen carefully. For the time being, nothing means anything to me: security of existence, prospect of a career, the treasures of culture, of spirituality, of education. Even law studies mean nothing to me for now, and I want to tell you that even my entire life means nothing to me for the time being—while this people lives in such terrible outer and inner misery. As long as this folk has no culture, no intellectuality, and no secure existence, I too will possess none of all these goods. Hopefully you understand what I mean, Gerkenrath."

The friend shrugs his shoulders. "Of course I understand! I just mean, Wessel, you will realize that one does not bring culture to these people, and to people in general, by brawling around for life and death and–"

Almost cheering, Horst Wessel shouts, "Yes, you do! Exactly like that! Why, now we are getting to the heart of the matter. Don't you think that I know exactly how many intellectuals feel repelled by our rough manners and our rough language and our entire rough presentation? Hans, this must be, simply has to be! The house must first be built before it can be furnished. Roads have to be built before you can drive cars on them. First the political existence of this fatherland must be secured under all circumstances, before we may once again think of Goethe, Hölderlin, Johann Sebastian Bach and of all the things which gladden the soul. Gerkenrath! There is no German culture without a German state and there is no German state without a German people.

"You know I never bother with phrases. And I have just told you a fundamental premise of my world view. And now I'm going to tell you the application of that world view.

"It sounds a bit rough, but we got rough in battle. The practical application of this world view is as follows: he who is an intellectual German man–"

Horst Wessel interrupts himself and begins again, very slowly and very forcefully, as if wanting to ram this realization into his friend's head with hammer blows: "He who is an intellectual German man, who knows the cultural giants of this German nation and loves them all his life, who wants to guard and cultivate them, who wants to contribute his small or large part to their continued flowering and growth, who feels that they are the most precious possessions—it is precisely he, Hans, who must push them aside right now, in this present time. Because the house must first be cleaned for this culture, get it? Perhaps the house must first be rebuilt from the ground up.

"And when the house is there, proper and dignified, cleaned and clear through and through, then we're ready. Anyone who is convinced that today's German house is not worthy to house the true German intellectual goods must first get out of the theatres, out of the salons, out of the study rooms, out of the parental homes, out of literature, out of the concert halls—and do you know where he has to go? He must go out into the streets, he must go into the midst of the people, must speak and shout and, if need be, lash out, so that the old, ramshackle German house is torn down and a new one can be built."

Horst Wessel beams at Gerkenrath from two bright, hot eyes.

"You see," he says quietly, "that's how things stand. And as paradoxical as it may sound to you, Hans: in these proletarian quarters where I stay, in these wretched castles of despair, misery, crime, woe, and incitement, in these districts where you have certainly never been before, but which have become my home, even if you turn up your intellectual nose a hundred times—here German culture is being defended by us, by the SA, that culture, my dear one, which you only want to possess, but for which you do nothing to preserve it.

"I tell you: every little brawl with a communist on some street corner, every little march of the SA in a savaged area, every hall fight is a step forward on the road of German culture, and every head of an SA-Man beaten in by the Commune has been held out for the folk, for the Reich, for the house of German culture.

"You see, I can explain to you exactly what it is all about, precisely because I am an intellectual person. And I do my SA service day after day, night after night, as long as necessary. I want to be nothing other than a foot soldier of Adolf Hitler. I want to brawl with communists as much as I can. And I tell you, I want to fight them hard, without holding back!

"I know that there are university professors and writers and painters and musicians who are said to be the guardians and bearers of this country's cultural goods. Right now that is not true. At the moment, the guardians are the nameless men who put up posters and distribute leaflets, who protect the halls of our assemblies, who become unemployed, who starve and thirst and freeze and beg, who risk their health and their lives each hour.

"Dear Hans, in times when fates have to be decided on a large scale, sometimes one has to do very primitive things. Just as man must eat to be able to work, so we must fight, fight primitively and archaic, to secure the nation.

"Because the SA is marching for Goethe, for Schiller, for Kant, for Bach, for the Cologne Cathedral and the Bamberg Horseman, for Novalis and Hans Thoma, for German culture, believe it or not.

"They want Germany to become completely German again, that is, to become National Socialist. Either that succeeds or it does not. But it must succeed. And it will succeed with this SA, which you look down upon because it is fighting in the streets. You know Hyperion, don't you! They don't know it. And because I know him, I want to help to ensure that Hölderlin will walk over German soil many more times, but first he must find German soil, and I will help him prepare it, and that is why, my dear fellow student, that is why I am marching through Friedrichshain with a hundred wild and robust lads, and punching every Communist in his trap. Period. Finished."

Dr. Gerkenrath sighs a little impatiently. "Dearest Wessel," he says, "it may well be so. But I just can't imagine that, even in a roundabout way, these wild fellows from Wedding have anything to do with German culture, that you pay homage to Goethe with your bloody hall fights, and that you are bearers of culture with your loud, provocative screaming and your uncouth, terrible manners. And that you in particular throw away everything that—"

"Oh Gerkenrath!" Wessel answers calmly, "there is a widely cited phrase that you yourself like to use. It goes: *'Throw away so that you do not lose.'* So we are in the process of throwing away ourselves, the SA, so that we do not lose, but regain, and you stand by and watch and find that highly ungentlemanly, highly uncouth—yes, my goodness, fighting is not a very refined affair, but one can no longer defend German culture with fountain pens and typewriters, much less reconquer it. Now, my dear fellow student, we have to work for Goethe with beer mugs and chair legs. And once we have won, well, then we will again spread out our arms, press our cultural goods to our hearts and enjoy them."

Wessel remains silent and looks at his friend calmly, and then he must smile, as he sees him standing there, elegant, with well-groomed hands that now light a cigarette, with fine silk linen and a magnificent bow tie.

"Gerkenrath!" he suddenly says, "when the Third Reich is here, you will have always said it will come, and you will walk around with the swastika and shout *'Heil Hitler'*—but you still won't have understood what I just told you. Perhaps then I will no longer be able to explain the whole thing to you again. Because you must not forget that we not only brawl for this German culture, but that we also die for it if we have to. And that is what puts us one step ahead of you. Heil Hitler!"

And with that Horst Wessel continued. Behind him, Dr. Gerkenrath took off his hat, slowly and somewhat annoyed. Slowly because he is very busy with the thoughts that his fellow student Wessel has just expressed, and annoyed because he finds many of these thoughts, whether he likes them or not, brilliant.

24

MURDER

In the Red Centers, people are working with dogged diligence. Especially in the Karl Liebknecht House they are brooding over a tremendously precise plan of attack. It concerns a special action, the execution of which is widely debated. Specifically, it concerns Storm 5 of the Berlin SA.

Storm 5 has become extremely dangerous. It appears to contain some of the most active, cunning, and passionate elements. They even know of some old, reliable communists who are suddenly abandoning the Red Front, only to reappear as brown shirts, joining the rank and file of Storm 5.

The Storm Leader is Horst Wessel.

And the Red Centers believe that something must be done to halt the growing influence of this leader and the growing power of his Storm.

So while these centers are racking their brains to come up with ways to deal with this Storm, both clean and dirty, Horst Wessel is racking his brains over an entirely different problem.

Actually it is quite a pretty and graceful problem—that of a brass band. He does not want a band like the other SA Storms and Standards have them, with beating drums and trumpets. No, the Horst-Wessel-Storm marches into the very midst of the Commune, so he needs to find something to tempt the communists, lure them to their windows, pull them to the front doors. Something which slightly annoys and tickles them at the same time.

What kind of marching bands do the Red Front troops have?

They have shawms!

Shawms, whose nervous and at the same time stirring sound reminds one of French clairons, maybe a tiny bit more subdued than them, but nevertheless a grand musical provocation, maybe for this very reason.

Shawms are forbidden in the SA. The SA does not use Red Front instruments.

Horst Wessel laughs to himself. But why not? They should! Exactly those instruments!

The Commune must be provoked, lured, and beaten by its own music. Shawms are easy to play, he thinks, and many SA-Men within Storm 5 already know the instrument from their time inside the Commune.

That's what we're going to do, the Storm Leader thinks, *so we better start collecting. I can't tell them about the plan ahead of time, so I'm collecting for an SA country lodge.* And so it happens.

Horst Wessel makes out many small receipts, in sizes of ten and fifty pennies, for an SA country lodge.

Many hundreds of these receipts were bought. As always, Storm 5 did its duty, although they didn't really get the purpose. Because building a country lodge would take more money than they could ever collect in a lifetime. Besides, they didn't even have the time to build one.

Well, after a few months the Storm Leader has collected a sufficient amount. And so, one evening the Storm comes across a dozen brand new instruments gleaming on their tables: shawms, shawms!

The Horst-Wessel-Storm marches through Red Wedding.

And everything happens just like the Storm Leader thought it would: everyone hurries to the windows, stumbles out of front doors, everyone comes running from the side streets, people gather to view them from the doorways. Only Red Front Fighters play the shawms, so that's who they're expecting, joyfully, and sympathetically.

And then a brown crowd turns the corner. It gets bigger and bigger, all of them marching in lock step. The swastika flag is waving above their heads and the crowd plays, shouts, cheers, and also plays on the shawms:

"Raise our flag, remain in close formation..."

The Horst-Wessel song!

The song of the National Socialist revolution!

On communist instruments!

The streets in Wedding observe this scene with long faces. Some of these long faces send short messages to the red headquarters.

And people in the red headquarters pull even longer faces.

Storm 5 of course.

The Horst-Wessel-Storm.

Horst Wessel!

And it is these two words that the thoughts of the Karl Liebknecht house get stuck on. There is a long discussion.

Once again the Zossener Straße lads are meeting at Father Mehl's place for a chat. They talk of the party convention and of Christmas, about their last stint in prison and the Young Plan.[44] In a nutshell, they know that the Young Plan will force German workers into sixty years of compulsory labor, and that is quite enough for them.

Father Mehl, who has been a PC and SA-Man for a long time now, goes downstairs to buy some bread rolls. The guys don't really want to let him go, because it is so damn cold and draughty. It is January 14th, right in the thickest of winter.

The old man waves away their concerns. No, no, he has sat around for long enough. And the boys are on night duty, so they can already freeze as long as they please. Besides, he wanted to stretch his legs for a bit, and winter air is supposed to be healthy.

Well, so they let him go. And Father Mehl steps away.

But before three minutes have passed, the doorbell already rings up a storm, and when Schulz rips open the door, they stare in amazement, at the old Mehl standing outside, gasping for air, unable to speak.

He must have raced up the four stairways as fast as he could. He doesn't have any rolls in his hand, and he looks terrible, completely pale, with thick veins pulsing at his temples.

Staggering into the kitchen, he stutters a bit, and with trembling, almost lifeless hands, holds a newspaper out to them. All of them are alert now—they realize that something terrible must have happened—something more terrible than a party ban or some kind of robbery. They bend over the paper in complete silence.

"Assassination attempt on National Socialist student!"

So screams the headline.

And underneath it:

"Shot down in his room."

And then they see a photograph. They all know this face, one as

---

[44] A new international agreement created in 1929, providing for an updated schedule of German reparation payments due under the Versailles agreements, which would be financed by American banks. The National Socialist government repudiated these debts upon their rise to power.

well as the other. There is no need to read any further; they stand up and the paper rustles to the floor.

Horst Wessel murdered.

In their minds, they keep repeating those three words. They are not weak nor soft people. They are neither sentimental nor particularly nervous. For a long time now they have been watching the work of the Storm 5 leader in the riskiest and reddest Berlin districts with respect and trepidation in equal measure. It was to be expected that the Commune would one day take revenge on him for this work. They imagined this revenge to take place in a brawl or an actual clash in the open street. But that they would shoot down Horst Wessel like a dog, cowardly shooting him in his own room, in this vile, criminal manner... this brave, young, decent man did not deserve this. Their comrade did not deserve this.

Silently, they walk down the stairs, head for the news stand at the corner and buy everything they can. They spend today's dinner money on newspapers.

How could they eat, anyway? And then they read all the gruesome details, one by one and every single one of them with clenched teeth.

It's true, he was shot down like a dog.

As vile and cowardly as only criminal vermin can get.

But they also read that he is still alive. The shots of his murderers, the red-front pimp Ali Höhler and the Jewess Cohn went right through his jaw. The landlady wanted to fetch a Jewish, communist doctor, but with his last bit of strength Wessel waved her away.

That evening, SA-Man Schulz prays for the first time in years. Just two short, fanatical sentences.

Dear God, do not let Horst Wessel die.

Dear God, let us catch the murderers.

* * *

After six weeks of indescribable torture and inhuman pain Horst Wessel died. He was conscious for a few days. During this time, the Gauleiter brought him flowers and sat by his bed for a long time. His comrades greeted him silently, their arms raised, their minds deeply shaken. On February 23rd, at half past six in the morning, he closed his eyes forever.

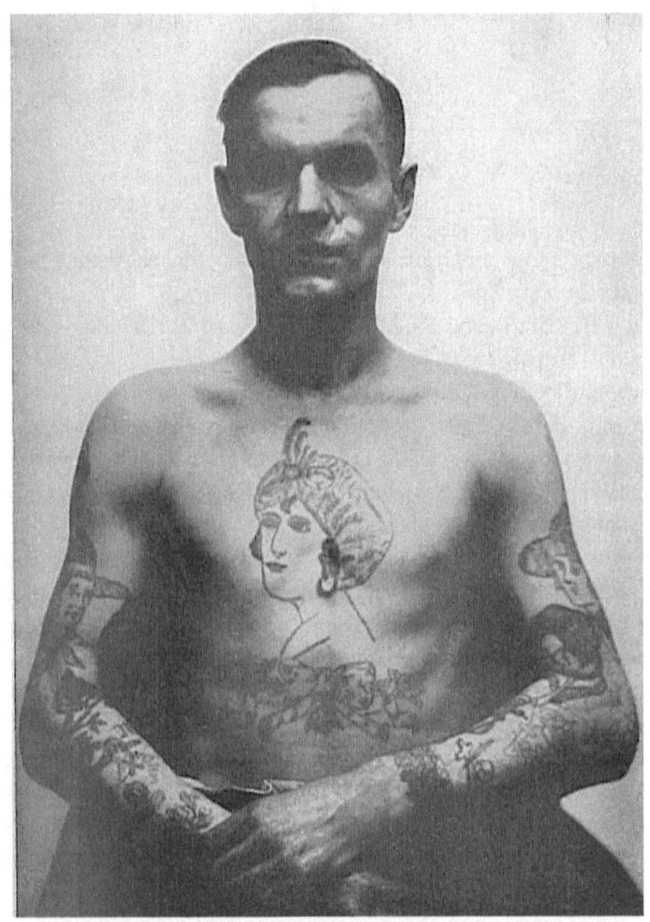

The communist Ali Höhler, who murdered Horst Wessel.

25

MARTYR

The very same morning at eight o'clock, ten thousand people in Berlin are in mourning.

And while the Berlin SA holds a silent vigil at the murdered man's coffin, Dr. Joseph Goebbels fights a tough battle.

At the police headquarters, people are being very cold.

"Do you think...," he is told by the irritable officials, "do you imagine we will allow you to hold a demonstration for every single person that gets shot? Moreover, in the Horst Wessel case, political motives are by no means established yet."

Furiously, Dr. Goebbels replies: "This is not a demonstration! We are laying to rest the creator of our song, our anthem, who was cowardly assassinated by the Commune! A burial! And the entire party is bound by honor to accompany the martyr on his final journey! It is our duty!"

The gentlemen at Alexanderplatz just shrug their shoulders. They have been instructed to reject absolutely any plan in honor of the deceased. Mr. Bernhard Weiss knows exactly what Horst Wessel means to the Berlin SA. He is also very much aware of his own standing among the SA, repaying their hatred and contempt as best he can.

A funeral procession of ten carriages is all that's conceded, for the relatives, the Gauleiter, a total of thirty people. Not a man more.

"And flags? Flags? We are very sorry, but we cannot allow the coffin to be covered with a swastika flag. Decorating the coffin with a party flag is a provocation. We forbid it."

That's too much for Dr. Goebbels.

He jumps up, banging his fist on the table. His face dark red with rage, he unleashes thunder against the gentlemen of the police, who are listening speechlessly.

"We are used to giving honorable burials to our dead, gentlemen. Do not think for even a second that you can rob this murdered man of his honor by forbidding his friends to pay their last respects! Very well! You even forbid him to be buried under the flag for which he died. We have not the slightest intention of burying the flag with him. It shall wave over our heads as we march forward across the graves!"

And with that he gathers up his belongings, slamming the door behind him. The gentlemen wince.

"Theatre!" one of the detectives consoles himself.

"Well," the head of department hesitates, "I'm not so sure. I don't like the look of this. But an order is an order after all."

And that settles the matter for our gentlemen in the police headquarters.

But it is not settled for Berlin.

It is not settled for the SA.

And it isn't settled for the Commune either.

*　*　*

On March 1st, Horst Wessel is led to his final resting place.

On this day, the entire German Berlin has gathered along the route of the funeral procession. Silently mourning, shoulder by shoulder, they form an impenetrable, black wall.

Not a word is said. No shouting can be heard.

And then the funeral procession approaches—it is truly not pompous.

One carriage with a simple coffin, almost disappearing under wreaths and flowers. Behind it a second carriage with the mother of the deceased.

Thousands and thousands of hands slowly rise, and under these arches of grief and love the coffin moves along.

One can only hear the soft scratching of the wheels, the slow hoof beat of the horses and every now and then a restrained sob from the crowd lining the road.

Never before has German Berlin given one of their dead a more dignified, more poignant escort. A student is buried, an SA-Man by the name of Horst Wessel, nothing more. But he is one of their best, he fought for them on the front lines, and although his voice may have died down, his song has not. And in the hearts and minds of these thousands, his song softly reverberates as the coffin passes them by.

But they are not the only ones unable to forget the dead man's song. The communists are there as well, positioning themselves in front of the cemetery. Even in death, they hate this man with a passion. As the first carriage turns the corner, a brutal howl breaks loose from their crowd, quickly followed by a volley of stones hurled towards the funeral procession.

"Down with the bloodhound!"

"Down with the criminal Wessel!"

"Smash the coffin to bits!"

"Pimp!"

"Rent boy!"

In the carriage following the coffin, a pale woman looks out in horror.

Why is there so much noise outside? What are these people shouting?

Very soon, Wessel's mother, who goes to bury her beloved son, the son she gave for Germany, will have to endure the faces of the most disgusting lot she has ever seen.

They come closer, raving and roaring in dense crowds.

The pale woman now clearly hears their shrieking calls.

"Hand over the coffin!"

"Smash the lid!"

"On the street with this deadbeat!"

The small funeral procession comes to a halt. It remains stunned under a wild avalanche of whistles, cussing, stones, and curses.

And now the hordes are approaching. Within this very minute, their unclean, criminal hands will touch the wreaths and flowers covering the coffin, and then...

The men in the funeral procession turn pale with boundless rage.

No SA is around to help, no police appear...

But there it is, at the last second, saving Berlin from its tremendous shame. Rubber truncheons fly into criminal faces, allowing the carriages to continue.

Slowly the coffin turns into the cemetery. Here too, thousands of people have been waiting for hours. SA and student corps line the driveway. The students' flags and rapiers are lowered, the arms of the SA are raised, and through their midst they carry the coffin, now covered with a swastika flag and Wessel's student cap.

The day is grey and gloomy. Flags stand motionless by the crypt. Lifeless cloth clings to their shafts.

A number of eulogies are delivered. Orators include the two pastors of St. Nicolai, representatives of the two student corps which Wessel belonged to, then the Supreme SA commander Pfeffer[45] and finally Dr. Joseph Goebbels.

Just as the immortal verses of "The Good Comrade"[46] are sung, as the flags are being lowered, as sobbing and crying breaks out at the graveside, during this utterly pious farewell, all hell breaks loose once again: shrill whistles pierce the air, stones are thrown over the wall, and the Internationale drowns out the SA's requiem.

Women break down. Horrified men duck down behind gravestones. People can be seen fleeing across grave mounds, between the cypresses and wooden crosses.

The SA is standing, but their jaw muscles protrude like ropes; their lips have turned into narrow lines. Single tears, filled with the most irrepressible rage and shame trickle down more than one cheek. The SA stands unmoving.

Deep down they know, know it with every last muscle fiber in their clenched fists, that right now not only the dignity of their dead comrade's burial is at stake, but also that this is a test of their entire movement. They will not disgrace this solemn ceremony. They stand in undying loyalty, unmoving. They will stand and continue their motionless vigil, even if they should be slain one by one at this open grave.

And they begin to sing. It is the dead Horst Wessel's song, and it has taken on a new tonality—massive, heavy and threatening: "Raise our flag..."

Thousands are singing along. They are about to witness something strange, almost unreal. After the song ends, Dr. Goebbels gives his obituary. He closes with these words:

"And you shall rise again..."

At this moment the sun breaks through the clouds. Formerly lifeless flags suddenly start to wave from their shafts, although not a breath of wind can be felt. All of this only happens within seconds.

---

[45] Franz Pfeffer von Salomon was a Freikorps fighter renowned for his resistance activities against the French occupation of the Ruhr area. The first SA commander after its reestablishment in 1925, he was dismissed from his command in 1930 after his loyalty was called into question. Expelled from the NSDAP in 1941, he died in 1968. Although his name would suggest otherwise, he was not Jewish, hailing from a family of German nobles.

[46] "Der Gute Kamerad" (sometimes known as "Ich hatt' einen Kameraden") is a traditional lament of German armies often sung at military funerals, written by Ludwig Uhland in 1809.

But everyone saw it: For these few seconds, the red swastika flag suddenly lit up, burning brightly in the sun.

A shiver went through the crowd.

And it is as if God had decided to send his holy breath across the open grave and the flags, to bless the fallen and all those who belong to him.

Communists attack Horst Wessel's funeral procession.

Horst Wessel is laid to rest at St. Nikolai cemetery in Berlin.

26

Escape

Now comes a time of war. A bitter, determined war against the police and the Commune.

The movement's casualty lists are growing lengthier by the day. The Berlin party has already counted over a hundred fallen comrades in its book of the dead.

The war is no longer lively and open, as it was in the beginning, with great brawls, great victories, and honest skirmishes in the streets.

That part is over. The Commune has stopped visiting their assemblies a long time ago. They understood that NSDAP gatherings and their stewards are not to be trifled with.

Instead, the Commune has begun to organize a substitute for these brawls. Their focus has shifted towards a cowardly and insidious conflict, defined by sudden attacks and lightning-fast murders, a guerrilla war in the darkness and remote deserted streets.

A dagger flashes for a second. A shot whips across the road. A dead man lies on the pavement.

There is not much the SA can do against these brigand-style assaults. Occasionally they send a commando squad into areas where a particularly cowardly murder has been committed on one of their own. These commandos roam the streets, picking out one, maybe two and sometimes even whole squads of communists. Then they administer the appropriate level of beatings to the communists. It is a serene, almost orderly affair. Nothing more and nothing less.

Sometimes this procedure buys them a few days of peace, sometimes a few weeks. But sooner or later there's always another SA-Man lying in the street, either stabbed in the back or shot from behind.

It is a bitter feud, nameless and desperate, an insidious affair that disgusts the SA. They do not understand this type of fighting. The Commune introduced it, and the SA will not sink to their level.

But they fight tooth and nail to defend their skin.

And they are growing increasingly bitter.

Schulz walks through Jewish Switzerland.[47]

This particular area consists of a number of residential blocks around Dragonerstraße, where the Eastern Jews are busy working on their springboards to a Berlin career. Here they are still extremely modest and suspiciously eager to please. Very busy, very greasy characters in greasy clothes, with greasy manners and greasy occupations. Later on, years from now, they will drive drown Kurfürstendamm in their own cars, laughing at dirty jokes in the evening revues like the made men they have become.

Schulz doesn't mind all of this too much—he is just passing through.

He is on his way to Haberland's halls, because they are having a Storm evening today. Haberland Storm evenings are always swell.

Mostly because they are right in the middle of enemy territory, which has a special charm for any real SA-Man. Because everyone who goes to Storm evenings in the Haberland's ballrooms is putting his life on the line. No one who goes there can guarantee that the next morning he will wake up in his own bed, safe and sound. All of them are prepared to experience that morning in a hospital bed or at a rescue station... if they live to see the next day.

At half past eleven the Storm evening is over.

And a familiar feature appears on all of their faces, Schulz included. Their faces become hard, revealing some vicious smiles. Because now begins the decisive part of their assembly, of the entire evening: getting home.

They turn up their jacket collars to hide the brown shirt underneath. The caps disappear into pockets and off they go, in groups of two or three people.

At this point they are no longer recognizable as SA-Men. They look like everyone else in this part of the city, returning home at around twelve o'clock. Men, young and old, cigarettes between their lips, hands in their pockets. But their looks do not help them. There must be something about the way they carry themselves. It is difficult to

---

[47] Nickname given to an area of the so-called "Bavarian Quarter" district in central Berlin, famous as the residence of several prominent Jewish intellectuals.

explain, but the Commune can sniff them out from three hundred feet away. Maybe it's in their faces, maybe their attitudes.

In Dragonerstraße, they meet the first assault. It follows the typical pattern of communist assaults during that time: twenty to thirty of these highwaymen break out of building entrances with brass knuckles, cudgels, hidden daggers, and revolvers.

And there is only one remedy.

Schulz alerts the three friends that are walking with him through some quick nudges and a brief shout. Then they chase away, closely followed by red thugs.

On light soles, the four of them sprint into Münzstraße. It is full of familiar faces, hundreds of them: pimps on all sidewalks, in front of each pub and every building entrance, caps pushed back, smoking cigarettes.

The whores standing by their side start screaming as they see the four SA-Men approaching, and the mob immediately understands what is going on and what they need to do. Because pimps and communists are pretty much indistinguishable in this area.

And so a wild chase starts, roaring communists behind them, waiting pimps in front of them. This damned street has turned out to be a trap.

But they are not going to lose heart, far from it. They are way too tough for that.

Schulz pulls an illegal revolver from his trouser pocket and fires four warning shots towards their pursuers.

The bandits scatter, and this brief moment of confusion is enough for the four of them to return to Haberland's ballrooms, safe and sound.

And though their breathing is still a little ragged, Schulz and Hermann, Gohrs and Ede are grinning happily.

Well then. They're in good hands here. But they know very well that the shots fired by Schulz will cause some inconvenience later on. Within the next fifteen minutes in fact. Because the Commune works fast. They are going to denounce the four of them with a quick telephone call to the nearest police station, and in a few minutes the riot squad will arrive. Not to deal with the communists, but to check the SA for weapons.

Nothing new here.

Schulz takes aside Hertha, the waitress. Twenty-one years old, a natural blonde without any hydrogen peroxide, just as sensible as any man, except for maybe a few dreamy glances at SA uniforms.

She understands immediately.

A revolver disappears into the piano, a pistol in the ladies' room.

"Let's have some beers," says Schulz, "and some cheerful songs. Remember, we've been sitting at this pretty table for three hours now. And we are celebrating a birthday, doesn't matter which one, any one will do."

And so they start celebrating.

Hermann starts off with his clean, hoarse cantus: "*...and he wants to climb back down... and he couldn't from that place... and already the ravens... hack him in the face... So you see... that's what you get...*"

Schulz wants to hear his favorite as well, the "Argonnerwaldlied": "*Argonne Forest at midnight... a pioneer stood on guard...*" But suddenly the door is torn open, and the riot squad comes rattling inside.

Behind the officers' stern faces, they count two, three, five communists in total. Cohrs recognizes one of them immediately. He has had the pleasure of beating him up not quite eight days ago.

So he's in? Then things could get dicey.

And they do get dicey.

This time the officials are particularly hard-working, thorough, and snappy. They tip over each table and every chair. They crawl into every corner. Every trouser pocket, every jacket lining, every waistcoat pocket gets frisked. Cohrs is waiting patiently for the inevitable moment.

Which promptly arrives. The once-beaten communist walks up to the commanding officer and points at Cohrs.

"Lieutenant... this boy here was the one who shot at us... that's him... I've seen it with my own eyes."

The officer briefly turns to Cohrs. "What is your name?"

"August Wilhelm Cohrs. I did not shoot. I don't even have a gun. I've been sitting here for hours by the way, and nobody did any shooting in here."

"We'll see about that in a moment," snarls the officer, "step aside. Constable, take down his personal data."

The constable draws his notebook. "Name? Place of residence? Employment?"

Next to the officer stands the communist, also holding a notebook. With a sardonic grin he too writes down all the details. Name and address. That's the way they're filling in those secret Nazi lists kept at the Karl Liebknecht House.

Cohrs is extremely indifferent to all of this. He watches the investigation continue. They don't find the revolver in the piano, but unfortunately the gun in the ladies' room resurfaces in the hands of a young policeman.

The lieutenant violently snaps at Cohrs.

"This is your gun, isn't it? Don't even try to deny it; this is the gun used in the shooting. Look here, four cartridges missing, all right. So let's hear it, does this gun belong to you or not?"

Cohrs doesn't say yes, and he doesn't say no. That's a neat little trap he's fallen into. If he says yes, he goes to prison. If he says no, he'll get a comrade in trouble.

So he remains silent.

"Arrest." As one of the officers is getting ready to lead Cohrs outside, something strange happens.

During all of this, a lonely man has been sitting in the far corner of the room, a glass of beer in front of him, not paying any mind to the SA people and officers barging in.

Hertha knows him, and right away she let Schulz know that they wouldn't have to worry about him.

Now all of a sudden this man calmly gets up, phlegmatically addressing the policemen. "Would you please show me the gun?"

The lieutenant responds cuttingly: "What? Why? What's your business here? Who are you?"

The man smiles complacently. "The owner of that weapon there."

The officers, communists, and the four SA-Men are pulling some exceedingly stupid faces, staring in amazement at the gentleman and his statement. Has he gone mad?

But the man calmly proceeds in his explanations, "You see, I wanted to shoot myself this evening. I fired four test shots, and with the final cartridge left inside I wanted to kill myself. But then I changed my mind and deposited the gun in the ladies' room. I figured it wouldn't do much harm in there. Ladies don't kill themselves that easily."

The room is completely silent. The lieutenant feels embarrassed by this strange man's smug smile. His insides are churning with rage. This whole story is nothing but a lie, and a big one at that.

"Do you have a firearms license?" he asks brusquely.

"Here you go," the man answers, handing him a piece of paper. As the lieutenant reads his name, he clicks his heels, does a narrow bow and returns the license.

"Thank you."

Then he turns to his people. "Fall in!"

And turns to Cohrs. "You are free to go."

A rather astonished police squad leaves the place with five disappointed communists in tow. All they got were some names and SA addresses. But even that will be valuable in due course.

When Schulz and his friends have recovered from their amazement, the man who "wanted to kill himself" with their pistol has already disappeared.

"Now that was something," Schulz states.

Dead tired, they make it to their quarters that night.

27

ABUSE

A few days later Cohrs gets arrested again, this time together with his girlfriend Hanna. Schulz tried to protect them, but that went wrong and now all three of them are in trouble.

It was a thoroughly stupid affair, altogether superfluous and nonsensical. They might just as well have gone home in peace instead of being driven to Alexanderplatz, if only...

Well, if that thing hadn't happened.

More specifically: The assembly at Saalbau Friedrichshain. Dr. Goebbels is giving a speech. There are five thousand people in the hall and three thousand outside near the Fountain of the Fairy Tales. Everything is nice and tidy, except for a few small, insignificant arguments here and there.

All is well. Goebbels leaves. The hall bids him farewell with a giant roar of pure enthusiasm. Outside however, the supervising police captain decides to issue a thoroughly absurd order.

"As the speaker departs, all acts of demonstration are strictly forbidden! *Heiling* in particular!"

It is one of those utterly dumb orders, completely devoid of even the slightest hint of healthy law enforcement imagination, an embarrassment that afflicted more than one of the commanding police officers of that period. When giving an order, one should be absolutely sure of one's ability to execute it, if necessary by force.

Does this incompetent, weak-minded police captain actually believe he can prevent the *Heils* of three thousand people? Dr. Goebbels has barely left the hall before a thunderstorm of *Heils* greets him on the street.

The police immediately lose their composure.

Rubber truncheons are brought to bear all over the place, those rotten, vile, entirely unworthy weapons used by an equally untalented and perverted police force to administer their fair share of justice to the German people. It should be noted as no small matter that within the Third Reich, these animalistic weapons were held in contempt and accordingly removed from daily life. During that period, however, not even high-ranking police officers were ashamed to slam this animalistic prop onto the heads, shoulders, and backs of their patient subjects.

And so they did.

There is tremendous roaring and shouting, a terrible confusion within the crowd. The undeniable genius of the police to turn a calm, albeit somewhat agitated crowd of onlookers into an inextricable tangle of screaming, beating, pushing, and fleeing people is proving its worth once again. And now the assembled police force starts mercilessly thrashing this tangle of helpless, scattered people. Cohrs is caught by a sergeant twisting back his arm in a painful police grip. Cohrs shouts something indistinguishable, which nevertheless seems to fit the whole situation perfectly.

He is arrested.

At that very moment he witnesses his girlfriend Hanna, completely wedged in between different people, being pushed against the police captain's back. The captain is 6 feet 2 inches tall, while Hanna stands at 5 feet 3 inches.

But the captain immediately turns around on his heel, deep red with anger.

"Arrest! Here! Arrest! That bitch hit me!"

Right away two officers jump the astonished woman, their rubber truncheons raised. Schulz has also been watching the scene. And that's one step too far for him. These gentlemen police officers, these officials whose job it should be to restore calm and order rather than lose their nerves in difficult situations, these uniformed jitterbugs go against the very nature of our old and experienced street fighter and SA-Man Schulz.

This is too much. He saw exactly that this girl could not help it at all. She didn't plan to touch the captain's precious back; she was simply pushed against him. Furiously, Schulz tries to work his way towards them. But he doesn't make much progress, because these police madmen have just started a new attack, pushing back the crowd towards the next street corner.

"I am a witness!" Schulz yells bitterly at an officer who tries to stop him. "I have a statement to make!"

"Shut it!" replies the officer and throws him back into a group of people.

All right, thinks Schulz. He wades across the sea of people, allowing them to carry him back to Friedrichshain where Hanna and the police captain are still standing. Then he dashes over the embankment and is left standing face to face with the police officer.

Indignant and angry, he starts his speech: "Captain, I have a statement to make! I demand to be taken to the precinct! This woman here is completely innocent!" But sometimes circumstances align to trick people into devious results. Just as Schulz has uttered these sentences, Hanna tears herself from their grip and runs away in fear. Three officers storm after her. Just as she is about to disappear back into the crowd, they grab hold of the girl. Schulz immediately runs after them, and now he is standing next to Hanna, when suddenly a policeman turns pale with rage as he sees Schulz.

"You again?" he yells at the SA-Man. "I just brought you to the corner!"

"I'm a witness!" yells Schulz.

"Shut up! Keep moving!"

"No!"

"I said keep moving!"

"No!"

"Come with me!"

And right away SA-Man Schulz is smashed onto the pavement in yet another police grip.

"Since when are witnesses arrested and beaten?" shouts Schulz.

But then he feels a slam against his skull, like a crack running through his brain and a sudden, razor-sharp toothache in all his teeth. Then he loses consciousness.

*　*　*

Fifteen minutes later he wakes up on a police truck. Cohrs and Hanna are sitting next to him.

And as the two SA-Men find themselves on yet another trip to Alexanderplatz, their sense of humor returns. As the car enters the red courtyard, general cheerfulness abounds, muffled only by a nice headache.

During the interrogation Schulz protests immediately.

"I have come forward as a witness! You can't arrest a witness! I demand to testify immediately."

The constable laughs.

"Oh no, lad, the things you ask for? Now, at half past midnight?"

"Then at the very least I'd like to know why I was arrested!"

"Don't make such a fuss!" the irritated officer interrupts him. "You'll find out in the morning. For now let's get you into a cell."

The officers empty his pockets. His comb, money, cigarettes, matches, and the rest of his belongings are piled up on the guard's table.

"And now the braces, man. It's the law, you know that."

Afterwards, the officer behind the table looks our two comrades up and down. He rocks his chair back and forth a few times. A broad grin appears on his face.

"So now what? What kind of cell are you in the mood for? To the communists or the apolitical ones? It's free choice in here. Take your pick!"

Schulz gives no answer.

For that is pure and naked mockery mixed with a bit of private sadism on the part of Mr. Guard over there. But after all, wolves are still more bearable than hyenas, so... He growls something incomprehensible, meaning apolitical.

And so they are led into a cell with six felons. At five in the morning they are awakened. Schulz would have loved to sleep an hour longer, and so he keeps growling something along the lines of, "What a damned mess."

The first interrogation is short. Once again name, occupation, address, and so on and so forth. It's obviously just a bit of chicanery.

At ten o'clock that day they are taken to police prison II. They still have no idea what they are being accused of. Unfortunately they also have no idea where Hanna is. When he tried to ask, Cohrs was flat-out refused an answer.

They are led into Cell 9.

* * *

After two hours of sitting around, the interrogation recommences. This time they are presented to the Political Department.

"Well then," Schulz grumbles excitedly, "at least we'll finally get to know what they're arresting us for." Cohrs is taken into a room on the left while Schulz takes a right-hand turn.

"You tried to free a prisoner during the Friedrichshain riots," reads the interrogating officer. "Is this correct?"

The room starts spinning before Schulz's eyes. So that's what's happening! Well, Hanna ran off while he was around... freeing of prisoners... cheers then... that's prison.

It is shaping up to be a long investigation. Hanna is brought in. The captain who Hanna is alleged to have beaten appears. So does the sergeant who arrested Schulz. At the trial in the afternoon, the judge finally asks the decisive question: "Captain, did you get the impression that this woman was beating you?"

The captain looks a bit uncertain and hesitates for a long time, before he explains indecisively: "Actually, I didn't feel anything. I only noticed that something was hitting my back."

"There you go," interrupts Schulz with satisfaction, "that's just what happened. The crowd pushed the lady against the Captain's back, that's all! When they tried to arrest her for that, I offered to act as a witness."

The constable, called as the main witness, bolts upright to testify: "I saw exactly how the lady raised her right arm and punched the Captain in the back."

Hanna protests immediately, extremely upset about this statement. The captain shakes his head slightly; he feels uneasy about the whole affair. But upon further questioning, the constable simply swears on his oath of service.

"This is outrageous!" Schulz is furious. His friend Cohrs looks very pale in his bench. But the judgment turns out to be bearable. It only lists a physical insult, dictating a forty mark fine for Hanna.

Shame crosses the girl's face in a red hue. She looks coldly at the judge and responds quietly, but with a deep bitterness: "And for something like that you lock me up with prostitutes and thieves."

A constable takes her gently by the arm and leads her outside.

"Now let's talk about your case," says the magistrate, and Schulz audibly clears his throat. He stands up.

"So you claim to have been a witness. But there is a charge against you—not for releasing prisoners; we shall drop that one. You are accused of resisting state authorities. So you resisted arrest?"

Schulz frowns. "Resisting arrest? What do you mean?"

"According to constable Urban, you walked particularly slowly. We consider this to be an act of resistance against state authority."

His mouth agape, SA-Man Schulz stares at the judge for a moment.

He can no longer control himself. This reasoning is just too absurd. And so he breaks out into resounding laughter.

His sentence: a forty mark fine as well, and five days in prison in case he doesn't pay the fine.

Schulz is released.

The trial against Cohrs on the following day is not as bad as he had imagined it. They acknowledge that he did not try to free any prisoners. Accordingly, he is sentenced to a total of ten days in prison.

28

Duty

And after two weeks everyone is back. Schulz, Cohrs, and Hanna are off on new assignments.

These new assignments are actually ancient ones and go by the names of: electioneering, marches, newspaper distribution, leaflet propaganda, chapter evenings, assembly protection, followed by more marches and assemblies, collecting donations, and house propaganda. Simply put, this means: running around in uniform day and night. It also means SA service, SA service, and SA service again.

And on November 14th they get a wonderful receipt for all of their hard work, all the sacrifice and devotion, for all the tired bones, sleepless nights, and unending enthusiasm: 108 members of the NSDAP move into the German Reichstag! From twelve to 108 in just two years! Not too shabby!

When Schulz hears of this result on the street, his joy breaks forth in an almost frightful roar.

Once again he is noticed; the eyes of the law descend upon him. But as the police are strangely lenient that day, Schulz manages to evade arrest.

But on Christmas Day there is trouble in the new Storm pub. The SA are sitting together with a sense of foreboding. And they are correct. They have barely lit the wax candles on their little fir tree when they hear a bang outside. Window panes burst, shards whir around, and immediately there's another bang. Schulz feels a hard blow against his knee, followed by a sharp pain. Then he turns pale and slowly drops off his chair.

That was a thoroughly festive Christmas greeting from the Commune to Storm 11.

On the drive to the hospital Schulz regains consciousness. He is bleeding heavily, but that doesn't detract from his indestructible cheerfulness.

Half-consumed with wound fever, he talks to his comrades: "You see, man, 108 Reichstag delegates... it may not be the Third Reich... but it sure is something... something to be happy about..."

Lying on the hospital's operating table, he gets a little impatient. "Let's go already... doctor... just push the shrapnel out... I really want to get back to the Storm pub... it's finally Christmas... but just in the Storm pub... and..."

He doesn't get any further with his rambling, because after some initial surprise at this curious fella, the doctor carefully plants an ether mask over his face.

"No... come on... nooo...," Schulz mumbles, before his dissatisfaction gives way to deep, colourful clouds, rushing and thundering him to sleep.

* * *

This Reichstag is not going to last.

The decision is in the air, and the air feels like it does before a big battle.

The brown battalions march. Their lock step has become secure. Their faces exude boundless confidence.

During this time the war movie *All Quiet on the Western Front* is being shown in a Berlin cinema. It was produced by Laemmle, a German-American and an unscrupulous Hollywood film maker, notorious for his cheesy, pathetic, unskilled films. German soldiers are portrayed by cute, wimpy actors. Its entire message contradicts every notion of living, suffering, and dying on the Western front held and endured by the German front soldier.

Schulz receives a secret order which he enjoys immensely.

Schulz goes to buy white mice.

He acquires 150 of these cute, happy, excited critters, carrying them to his Storm pub in a large cardboard box with some holes cut into it for air.

The pied piper is welcomed by the assembled Storm amidst hellish cheer.

"Don't laugh," he tells them with a wink of his eyebrows, "those aren't regular mice. They are presently involuntary volunteers for Storm 11, all set to make their small contribution to history."

And then he carefully distributes the animals among his SA.

"Take care," he orders, "make sure no harm is done to the little ones... Eleven... twelve... You want twenty at once? What on earth for? ...For your little sister? ...Don't you know women are afraid of mice? ...Yours isn't? ...All right... here you go..."

The SA isn't marching against Mr. Remarque and not against Mr. Laemmle either. They leave this mission to the white mice.

Thousands of people have gathered at Nollendorfplatz, protesting against this flick.

The hall goes dark. Shortly after the "heroic epic" has begun to showcase the German front soldier, as imagined by Mr. Remarque and Mr. Laemmle, a tremendous spectacle breaks loose.

Suddenly freed from their cardboard prisons, the mice, furious with fear and anger, begin to assault the spectators, climbing up their legs, scratching and biting. It is an exhilarating and thoroughly satisfying mess. Not even a gun barrage could have achieved such great effect. The SA's roaring laughter drowns out the horrified screams. Their triple "Heil Hitler!" thunders against all walls.

For now the performance is over.

Two days later the film gets banned. Mr. Severing[48] bites his lips.

---

[48] Carl Severing, a Social Democrat politician and Interior Minister of Prussia, who defended the continued presentation of *All Quiet on the Western Front*.

29

REWARDS

Around Christmas 1931, a document arrives from Munich.

The document is addressed to the Standard Leader. The Standard Leader smiles, and after some mysterious preparations, Schulz is called to the Standard Leader in an unusually formal manner. "Gee," mumbles a confused Schulz, "no idea what that guy wants. Did I do something? Did I insult anyone? No, not really. What does the little general want with me?"

And he marches off to the Standard Leader, in a rather unpleasant mood.

When he arrives at the Storm pub, the whole Storm is already there.

Schulz is not happy. He was never one for ceremonial things.

And there's the Standard Leader.

"Platoon leader Schulz!"

"At your service!"

"Platoon leader Schulz, the Supreme SA Commander has appointed you Storm Leader. Storm 24 will be formed by combining your old platoon with the 5th platoon. My congratulations. I am convinced that you will lead your future Storm just as well as you have led your troop up till now."

And with a warm expression, the Standard Leader gives him a firm handshake. Schulz is standing there like he was bolted to the floor. For a brief moment his skull drones in all keys. Some dark spots circle before his eyes for a few seconds, followed by a strangely hot feeling somewhere near his heart.

And finally he comes to his senses and understands. Storm Leader! Leader of an entire, great Storm! He, the worker Schulz! And he will lead his old comrades, his old friends. There they are standing, one next to the other, all of them cheerful to no end: Father Mehl, Hans,

Hermann, Cohrs, Fritz, long Emil, cheeky Max, and all the others. Unbelievable.

* * *

The Republic is angry at Dr. Goebbels, so they stick him with a treason trial. Ever the calm one, the Doctor just shrugs his shoulders and proceeds to get married. Under a mountain of flowers, under Gothic arches and the living arches of outstretched arms, he walks towards the public registry. He's wearing a brown shirt.

The Führer has traveled to Berlin to act as his best man, so this is a huge day for the SA.

Looking back, they have to admit that it hasn't been an easy year. Thuringia, Braunschweig, the referendum[49]... not too popular with the left-wing press.

But for the SA, everything worked out splendidly. As the year comes to an end, Germany counted two thousand Storms under flags, one hundred motorized Storms, fifty music troupes, two hundred marching bands, and 120 brown Standards! It has certainly been worthwhile. And it worked, even though the left-wing press had been very much looking forward to Captain Stennes and his little coup,[50] that man who wanted to turn the SA into a mercenary troop, with himself as its well-paid general. The press had been reeling with joy, showering the once-hated man with flattery and adulation! How beautiful it had imagined the course of events: Storm marching against Storm... SA against SS... Everything falling apart... Nothing but pieces and splinters... Forever. After all, the press argued, a mercenary troop belongs to the highest bidder... Goodbye National Socialism!

The journalists were very fond of what Stennes had to say: that he wasn't fighting against Adolf Hitler, but against the big shots.

And as they were pushing Captain Stennes to name one of the big shots, he named one who had already seen through his charade and thus seemed the most dangerous to him: Dr. Joseph Goebbels.

---

[49] In 1931 Thuringia becomes the first federal state in Germany to have NSDAP cabinet ministers, the SA holds a massive successful rally in the northern city of Braunschweig, and an NSDAP-backed referendum to dissolve the SPD-dominated Prussian Landtag is only narrowly defeated.

[50] The "Stennes Putsch" in 1931 was an unsuccessful attempt by Walther Stennes to splinter the SA in order to secure his own base of power within the National Socialist movement.

He should not have done that.

Because even though things went haywire for three days and the Berlin SA was left leaderless for the first and also the last time—this was the sentence that broke Mr. Stennes.

"What?" asked the SA, completely aghast, "our Doctor? A big shot?"

And the SA remembered the man who led the famous Spandau-Tegel-Reinickendorf-Wedding march where ten thousand communists had cordoned off the road. They remember the exact moment when their train stopped, the Doctor getting up in his car to overlook the situation. It was certainly not a laughing matter when he got out of the car, positioned himself right in front of the troupe of musicians and marched off into this raging and roaring hell scape. He marched onwards until they reached the veteran's association, where the police had blocked the street. Nobody has the power to make the SA forget something like that.

The Doctor, a big shot?

The man who took part in the hall battles, who comforted the wounded and accompanied the dead, who took large debts onto himself to give the Berlin party its newspaper... this man was supposed to be a big shot?

When the news reaches Schulz, he doesn't even get angry.

Usually he is easily excitable when it comes to people who he cares very much for. But this time, his reply is completely calm: "Very funny. That Stennes guy is a phony. Or he just got the wrong address. Maybe he wanted to join the Reichsbanner[51] all along. But definitely not the SA."

To Schulz, that was the end of it.

After a fortnight, the case was closed, and the whole thing vanished.

The SA's badge of honor was clean once again.

* * *

Slowly, they can feel a new time approaching. Very slowly.
Spring 1932.
A secret slogan is making the rounds in the SA. And even though

---

[51] The Reichsbanner Schwarz-Rot-Gold was the answer of centrist parties such as the SPD, DDP, and Zentrum to the proliferation of paramilitary groups in the Weimar Republic, intended to defend the young Republic against both the Left and the Right.

Storm Leader Schulz hears about it, his eternal front-soldier scepticism won't let him believe.

The slogan is short and sweet: This is the year that the Führer becomes Chancellor.

"No way," says Schulz, occasionally pausing to look up Reich Chancellor Brüning in a magazine, this pale, opaque, unapproachable face. "Things don't happen that quickly."

He secretly watches his boys. This slogan makes them seem almost feverish. Their faces are hot, and their thirst for action makes them look almost nervous.

The SA feels it in their bones, almost like one can feel an upcoming thunderstorm. A big decision is near.

But will it be the decision they are hoping for?

In his mind, Schulz weighs those heavy words, again and again:

Reich Chancellor Hitler.

Didn't they already predict that for the September elections in 1930? That was a year and a half ago. One and a half years of hard, bloody work. Will this really be the decision they've been waiting for?

*   *   *

It is a fierce election campaign which manages to unite thirteen and a half million votes behind the Führer. Thirteen and a half million! If this was a Reichstag election, they would have secured 220 seats.

How are they going to stop the NSDAP now? The SA is immensely confident.

30

REPRISAL

But then the thunderstorm comes crashing down on them. Three days after the election, Wilhelm Gröner, Reich Minister of the Interior and Defence, bans the entire SA.

In the Storm pub, the leader of Storm 24 is enthusiastic in the face of this catastrophe.

"Now we've done it!"

His comrades stare at him without the slightest bit of understanding. Has Schulz gone mad?

But Storm Leader Schulz, the old front soldier, is far from mad. His trench instincts are kicking in. Yes, things are going haywire right now. Their horizon is a wall of flames, smoke, fog, and destruction. But the trench warrior feels something: nevertheless, gentlemen, nevertheless... Precisely because of this, today is a good day. Let them come today.

He tries to explain it to his boys: "Of course it's madness what Gröner is doing. The system is mad. Just think about it. Can you just ban 400,000 men these days? Hell no, you can't. The Republic is not that big anymore! They no longer have that much strength! Now they're backed to the wall, you see? Now they're ready to risk it all. And that's where we win, you get it?"

But neither his Storm nor the SA in general are ready to see things his way yet.

Quite the opposite in fact. A wave of indignation sweeps through the Reich.

Again the police commence their sad work with an equally sad zeal; again the Brown Shirts have become outlaws. It seems as if the old 1929 days have returned in all their glory.

The next day, Schulz is in for a surprise. As he turns the corner, still very cheerful and confident despite the apparent catastrophe, he suddenly stops, as if rooted to the ground. His eyes close, then reopen again. His chin travels forwards. In short, he is gawking.

And what he sees in front of the Storm pub is definitely worth gawking at.

On the pavement, right in front of the Storm pub, there are beds waiting for him, eight beautiful bunk beds, neat and tidy, with straw mattresses, sheets, and pillows, first-class construction, as first-class as Schulz has ever seen among Storm pubs—a paradisiacal sight for a reserve sergeant in any solid guard battalion.

Littered around these beds there is a hopeless mess of pictures, brooms, buckets, boots, chairs, lockers, tables, and pots.

What happened here? Schulz wonders, as he uncertainly makes his way towards the strange sight. *Well, is it really that hard to comprehend?*

The Storm pub inventory is lying on the street. Now Schulz notices the swastika flag waving over the whole scene. He gets a little more cheerful. As long as the flag is still waving, things aren't over.

Although things do in fact seem to be over for the once beautiful Storm pub. Prussian policemen have closed down the pub, kicked the unemployed SA-Men back out onto the street, shortly followed by all of their furniture.

And that's why the beds and all of their stuff are now standing about on the pavement. The only thing Schulz is still wondering about is why the flag is still waving over the beds. He's not surprised by the laughing gawkers. After all, it's not every day that you get to see such neat soldiers' bunk beds standing out in the open Berlin streets.

As Schulz gets closer, he realizes why more and more people come running and start laughing.

Schulz sees that Hermann has installed himself in one of the upper beds. The insolence of it all leaves Schulz speechless. Hermann, the most creative joker of the whole Storm. This Hermann surveys the astonished audience from his elevated position.

Well-mannered as always, he has taken off his long boots and placed them next to the lower bed. He has also taken off his jacket, folding it neatly over the back of a chair with the brown tie on top of it.

He has tied the flag to one of the nearby bedposts, where it flutters merrily in the wind.

The two of them, Hermann in his castle and Schulz marching towards him, greet each other with a thunderous salute. Schulz is just about to climb onto another bed for a proper speech to the eaves-dropping crowd, when they are interrupted by the usual suspects.

Of course the police has to arrive at that very moment. It all happens rather quickly now. Before Schulz can get out a single word of his speech and before Hermann can put on one of his boots, their merry encampment has already been surrounded.

The amused audience is driven apart using the tried and tested rubber truncheon method. Then a truck rolls up, gets loaded with all of the SA's belongings, and drives off towards police headquarters.

"You see," remarks a content Schulz as they leave, "I might end up being right after all. Now it's just like during the first ban, at least that's what it looks like. But it's also different. Now they can no longer destroy us, no way! Our assemblies, our marches, they can't erase those with their rubber truncheons any more. It's pure despair."

As it turns out, the old trench warrior was right.

The ban only lasts until June 16th before it is lifted again.

The decree is announced at eleven o'clock in the morning. Five minutes later, Berlin is brown. Never before has the Reich capital seen so many brown uniforms on its streets. It looks like every SA-Man who got the news immediately hurried home to put on his brown shirt. And everyone seems to have taken time off to parade his brown uniform for at least an hour. Never before has the capital heard so many *Heils* than during those hours. The police has turned lenient once again. Some policemen even look at the brown shirts with amicable smiles. Is it possible that the heads under those shakos are finally beginning to understand?

At lunchtime, Berlin is fully decked with flags. Tens of thousands of large and small swastika flags hang from the windows and loft hatches, fluttering above the roofs. Storm Leader Schulz takes a long and proud walk with his friends.

But it does not take very long for the proud walks to end. Their SA work has started to become even harder.

As the first SA uniforms reappear in the streets, so do the shots of their red pursuers.

The Commune is frenzied, almost feverish. They organize downright hunts for SA-Men. The police publish brief reports on a daily basis:

SA-Man assaulted.
National Socialist shot.
Two SA-Men missing.
SA-Man found severely wounded.
SA-Man shot and killed.
SA-Man beaten and badly maltreated.
SA-Man stabbed to death.
National Socialists attacked.
SA-men shot from ambush.
SA-Man murdered.
SA-Man hospitalized with serious injuries.
SA-Man killed.
SA-Man left unconscious.
SA group pelted with stones.
Unconscious SA-Man hospitalized.
SA-Man shot.
SA-Man brutally murdered.
SA-Man beaten to death.
SA-Man stabbed to death.
SA-Man found with two severe abdominal injuries.
SA corpse pulled out of the water.
SA-Man killed with club.
Shot SA-Man found in Grunewald.
SA-Man thrown off tram.
SA-Man found mutilated.
SA-Man hospitalized after shot to the lungs.
SA-Man hospitalized after stabs in the back.
SA-Man found dead with wounds at the back of his head.

SA casualties are increasing at an alarming rate in those days.

Day by day, the hatred for the SA is growing more intense, destructive, and deadly, like an out-of-control wildfire.

The SA is resisting like never before. They are fighting a battle of annihilation, and all of them, every single leader and SA-Men alike share one conviction: if someone is to be annihilated in this battle, it will be the Commune.

The Commune, the Commune!!!

The policemen's faces, formerly mild and friendly, now exhibit smiles of utter helplessness and embarrassment.

The government is wearing the exact same smile. They remain

silent. The government is not helping its patriots in any way whatsoever.

The SA is alone. Depending only on their own strength, the SA-Men fight a crazed guerrilla war.

Eviction from an SA quarters after the SA ban

31

ELECTIONS

And once again there are elections!

These weeks demand much of the SA: utmost performance amidst extreme tension. To them, elections mean protection for assemblies, canvassing, propaganda service day and night, suicide commandos day after day, night after night.

Hundreds fall to those brutal weeks. The Storms are practically living in uniform.

Schulz has to go without sleep for almost fifty-two hours. Only the old front soldiers are able to endure such ludicrous efforts without keeling over.

Then comes election evening.

Sunday evening descends unto the city's artificial lights. Schulz and his men have gathered around the Storm pub's radio speaker. A tired group of pale, hollow cheeks, red-rimmed eyes, and shaky knees, every single one of them as exhausted as their Storm Leader.

But only on the outside!

They could lie down right away and sleep for eight days in a row. But they are waiting patiently for the first results.

Their hearts almost stop when the waltz music on the radio finally breaks off and the initial results are announced:

NSDAP 128,400 against 42,000
NSDAP 4,328 against 1,417
NSDAP 11,765 against 7,309
NSDAP... NSDAP... NSDAP...

At first, they *Heil* at each number, loud enough to cause the walls to shake with each newly announced vote count. Now, around midnight, they become quieter, more silent. They know that at this hour there are tremendous festivities at the Sports Palace, their party's great victory celebration. Dr. Goebbels is a key speaker. They are not going; staying in their old, modest storm pub instead. Why should they leave tonight? This is their home. They have slept many nights here in peace and security, while the Commune was waiting for them outside. This is where they brought their leaflets, piling them up before they set off to distribute them. This is where they had their little gatherings on endless evenings, rejoicing together when things went well and comforting each other when things went badly. It was here that they bandaged their comrades whenever one of them got hurt. Here they saw the pale lips of their wounded comrades stammer for water. Here they snarled at each other during arguments. Here they made friends for life, sometimes even until death. Here they ate, drank, and slept. It was more than a shelter. It was home.

And so there is no reason to leave home on this decisive evening. Here they want to hear the very last message, the final count. And finally, when they can hardly keep their eyes open anymore and have already grown much too tired for conversation, the clear voice of the announcer finally comes through the speaker:

"Ladies and gentlemen, we are pleased to announce the preliminary overall result. Mandates will be distributed as follows: National Socialists will receive 230 mandates..."

That's as far as the speaker will get this evening. A unanimous outcry blasts through the Storm pub, an almost choked cry of jubilant terror and immense pride.

230 seats in the Reichstag!

Almost fourteen million votes!

And thus the strongest party!!!

As the loudspeaker plays the "Deutschlandlied," the SA-Men of Storm 24 are standing in their modest Storm pub, dusty and tired men, young and old, their faces emaciated from countless exertions. Their limbs are dog-tired, their throats dry, eyes burning. And yet here they are, in clothes that have not come off their bodies for three days, with feet that are still aching from all the walking... Despite all of this, they are standing like a wall, suddenly awake and refreshed. Their eternal chorus, the holy anthem of life and death drowns out the Deutschlandlied:

Raise our flag, remain in close formation,
SA march on with calm and steady stride!
Comrades killed by Red Front and Reaction's ruination,
Today they march in spirit side by side!

A solemn silence follows. Without a word, they look at each other, these field soldiers of Adolf Hitler, every single one of them faithful until death. Schulz breaks the silence with an unspeakably hoarse voice, almost sobbing:

"Guys, guys... let's settle our election debts... I mean...," and his voice goes crazy with emotion, pride, and joy, "I mean...two hundred and thirty! ...Let's have a round on me!!! ...And another one, for the whole Storm! ...Jeez, man..."

And with that, his voice is gone completely.

* * *

That night, Storm 24 are sitting together long after midnight. There can be no talk of fatigue. And as morning dawns through the windows, Hermann jumps up on a chair, glowing face, and screams loud enough for his vocal cords to burst: "To our Führer, Reich Chancellor Adolf Hitler, three cheers... Hail Victory!—Hail Victory!— Hail Victory!"

Yes, how could it be otherwise? The Führer simply has to take over the government now. Not even Schulz doubts it any longer. Just like all the others, he remembers the old parliamentary custom to entrust the formation of a government to the leader of the strongest party. And so tomorrow Adolf Hitler will become Chancellor.

* * *

The morning comes and goes and at noon Adolf Hitler still hasn't been declared German Chancellor. An exception from traditional rules, he is offered the post of Vice Chancellor.

The Führer's car, parked in front of the Kaiserhof hotel, is surrounded by the SA. Rumors make the rounds. Allegedly even some of his closest confidants have advised the Führer to give in, that a bird in the hand is better than two in the bush, just as it has been the custom for all prudent, wise, and judicious people since time immemorial.

The SA is stubborn and does not believe in it. They haven't given up three hundred dead and thirty thousand wounded for this.

As the Führer leaves his hotel for a drive to negotiations in the Reich Chancellery, thousands of arms and hands of the loyal SA snap into position. They implore and plead. Thousands of shouts reverberate across the square: "Stay tough!"—"Führer, do not give in!"—"All or nothing!"

And for a moment, the Führer surveys his SA. He smiles, raising his hand in salute. And his masculine face shows an unforgettable determination.

The SA knows.

They know that this Führer of theirs does not know the word compromise. Neither does the SA. All is well.

32

VICTORY

At the height of summer, five Silesian SA-Men kill a Polish communist, a murderer and traitor to his country.

Earlier that year the government has issued an emergency decree imposing severe, harsh penalties on acts of political terror. Partially this is due to the insistence of SA leaders themselves, because the SA leaders have no desire to lose their best people to the cowardly, murderous manners of the Commune.

The five Silesian SA-Men are arrested and brought before a Special Court, one of those Special Courts which were intended to try Bolshevik murderers.

Without any central directive, a silent alarm goes through all SA Storms of the Reich.

Nobody has ordered them to do so, but on the day of the sentence they gather in their Storm pubs.

They know what "Special Court" means: death sentences.

It's life or death for their comrades.

The verdict is announced on August 22nd.

...sentenced to death...

...sentenced to death...

...sentenced to death...

Five accused, five death sentences.

A universal outcry goes through the SA, the party, and the entire Reich. Have the gentlemen of the Special Court completely lost their mind? Five men were fighting against Bolshevik madness, against the most diabolical, most destructive concept ever invented. Now they are supposed to lose their lives?

Understandably, Storm 24 is out of control. Like caged tigers, they keep roaming around the Storm pub. Until amidst all this uproar, Schulz utters one of his simple, naïve, and pious sentences: "Let it go.

Keep calm. The Führer will get them out."

And for a moment, his SA-men stare at him in shock and awe. Then they become a little quieter.

Meanwhile, the left-wing press stylizes the dead Bolshevik into something akin to a saint, while the five sentenced SA-Men are turned into sadistic beasts, to be put down immediately.

Right into this orgy of rage, hate, spite, and incitement, a telegram arrives. This telegram, posted in Munich, was received at the trial site in Potempa.[52] It was addressed to the five SA-Men sentenced to death, signed by Adolf Hitler. The telegram read as follows:

My comrades! In the face of this outrageous blood sentence I feel connected to you in infinite loyalty. From this moment on, your freedom is a question of honor to us. Just like we are duty-bound to fight against a government under which such a thing was possible.

Adolf Hitler

Schulz reads the telegram to his SA-Men. This time there is no cheering in the Storm pub. There are no comments by Schulz. In their hearts, however, this telegram has made their loyalty complete. The Führer had taken the fate of his five unknown SA-Men from Silesia into his strong hands.

Every word exchanged over this telegram is one too much. Their rage has died down. And even the smallest, slightest, most insignificant SA-Man suddenly begins to feel that his brown shirt, his brown cap, and the badge on his tie are guarantees that no one, whoever they may be, will be allowed to mess with them.

* * *

There is a new election, followed by more negotiations, and then another rejection.

Chaos has taken hold of the press, that poor, incited, and tormented instrument. Helplessness and indecision abound. Rumors are started, nourished, and abandoned. All kinds of coalitions are

---

[52] The 1932 Potempa murder trials convicted five SA-men of murdering Konrad Pietrzuch, a Communist trade unionist, by beating him to death in his home. All five men were released after the inauguration of the National Socialist government in 1933.

discussed and dismissed with incredible speed.

Lists of ministers are drawn up and torn again.

And finally the press announces that Germany has turned into a madhouse.

But for the SA, this is a time of great clarity. The weak ones run away, and that is good. Any lukewarm elements still left over disappear, and that too is good.

And once more, the SA stands cold and indomitable, like iron.

They keep quiet and wait. They are waiting for orders, whatever those orders may be.

Let them rack their brains in the mysterious halls of the high government and the dimly lit parlors of cliques and cronies. If Mr. von Schleicher[53] wants to negotiate with union representatives behind locked doors until his flabby mouth hurts, who are they to complain?

The SA is waiting, ready to march.

It may not have to march against Mr. von Schleicher—that would hardly be worth it or even necessary. But there still is an enemy to be destroyed. With one hundred seats, the Commune is still well represented in the Republic's Reichstag. That is their enemy, today just like yesterday. It has been their enemy for the past fourteen years.

And the SA is marching.

Once again they march towards the Karl Liebknecht House. The bloodthirsty banners are still hanging from its facade. Above, red flags are waving.

Ten thousand SA-Men encamp on Bülowplatz. They are silent, a tremendous threat ahead of the decisive battle. The brown soldiers look at the house, this giant hornet's nest, where for years murder after murder has been organized, where treason is committed, one assassination, uprising, and robbery at a time, without end.

They are watching this house very closely. They can smell the toxic fumes rising from every window in this Jewish communist headquarters. They glance into every window, towards the eaves, which seem so exceedingly well-suited for machine gun nests, to the massive, darkly threatening doors that close automatically at the touch of a secret button, to the narrow porter's windows that could

---

[53] Kurt von Schleicher was the final Chancellor before Adolf Hitler during the Weimar Republic. A former general, he aimed to control the NSDAP via a broad coalition of different parties with himself as the Chancellor. Resigning in January 1933 due to a lack of political influence and deteriorating health, he was killed during the Night of the Long Knives.

easily accommodate several gun barrels.

The SA considers all of this with experienced eyes, honed by years of street fighting. And even though the SA is not carrying any weapons, they can guarantee one thing: if even a single shot is fired today, not one stone of this pretty house will be left intact, and then the gentlemen with their whistling consonants and crooked noses will have to fry, like those separatists in the Pirmasens town hall back in 1924.[54] The SA is not in the mood for jokes.

But nothing is moving in the house. The windows are deserted, the gates empty, the roofs unoccupied. They only dare to murder at night.

The house is silent, even though Hitler's brown soldiers are standing right below its walls.

And then von Schleicher steps down, highly embarrassed.

Storm 24 arrives back at their quarters. Vacations have been cancelled. Storm Leader Schulz is not going easy on them. Because now it's all or nothing.

"I don't know anything," says Schulz, his lips narrow with determination. "I have no idea what the Führer is going to order us to do. But it's happening, you got that? And if anyone doesn't show up for duty..." He does not finish his sentence.

The last chapter meeting is on January 29th. And although it has been coming for a long time, nobody suspected that it would be of such importance. The hall is packed, and people are sitting together in feverish excitement.

The Führer is in Berlin, and crowds are piling up in front of the Kaiserhof Hotel. Negotiations are still going back and forth; that is all anyone knows.

This 29th of January 1933, a Sunday, is like a volcano waiting for its eruption.

Schulz overlooks the crowds assembled in the hall, a rough sea of people. The local group leader addresses a few words to them. And then suddenly Storm Leader Schulz is on stage.

For the first time ever, his comrades hear him speak High German, his voice cold with razor-sharp threat.

---

[54] Pirmasens is a mid-sized town in Rhineland-Palatinate, near the French border. In late 1923, a group of three hundred separatists moved into the town, occupying various public buildings against the will of the local government. Gathering additional troops, the separatists established a new local government, banning all other political assemblies. In February 1924 the local population rose up against them, burning down the separatist-occupied town hall. They regained control over Pirmasens, killing twenty-two people and wounding 158 in the process.

"Today we are but a party," he shouts, and his words fall heavy like hammer blows, "yet tomorrow we shall be Germany! Never before have I prophesied anything except that we will do our duty, whatever it may be, wherever it may lead us. But today, I will make one prophecy: Tomorrow Germany will be free. Tomorrow, that liberated Germany will have a Chancellor by the name of Adolf Hitler!"

It was the first and last speech Schulz would ever give in well-formed High German, and he held it to endless, ear-piercing jubilation.

The Horst-Wessel-Lied is sung. Not defiantly like in the past, but jubilantly, cheering for the things to come. After the assembly, nobody returns home. Instead, they march towards Kaiserhof in groups of four or five people. Not a single policeman tries to stop them.

As they march along, the modest Schulz feels pangs of remorse. He did give them something like a parole, didn't he? So what if everything turns out differently?

What if the Führer does not become Chancellor after all?

What if he leaves for Obersalzberg again, taking up the tenacious, dogged fight once more?

Then what?

Then Storm Leader Schulz has made a mess of things, a horrendous nonsensical mess. His forehead heavy with wrinkles and worries, he now marches through Wilhelmstraße.

But perhaps the Führer actually does become Reich Chancellor tomorrow! Then they could finally get some rest, he thinks, a great, festive holiday will come. Finally some time to think about something other than endless fighting and dying. He thinks back on the past seven years, remembering them with satisfaction. He has done his duty. In yet another war he has proven to be a good and faithful soldier.

In front of Kaiserhof, the SA tries to calm down the crowd.

"Go home, comrades... the Führer needs his rest... he'll have a hard day tomorrow... be reasonable..."

But the crowd does not move. They have been standing and waiting for many hours, and they will continue to wait even longer, until the next morning if necessary.

Again and again the "Deutschlandlied" rises into the night sky, then the "Preußenlied,"[55] followed by the proud song of the SA. An unending stream of *Heils* pelts the hotel windows.

---

[55] "The Song of Prussia" was the Prussian national anthem from 1830 to 1840, written by Bernard Thiersch in 1830 to honor the birthday of King Friedrich Wilhelm III of Prussia.

And suddenly Hitler is there, standing in an open window. The wide square trembles under thunderous cheers sweeping up towards his serious face.

* * *

As the evening of the next day, January 30th, 1933, descends onto the Reich capital, Wilhelmstraße has turned into a smoldering, blazing sea of torches. No one alerted the Storms. No one has gathered these hundreds of thousands. No one has paid for their torches, and no one has told them to march.

Their own hearts have alerted them to buy torches and march.

For on that day, the Führer Adolf Hitler became Reich Chancellor, the new head of the Reich.

Storm Leader Schulz can rest his conscience. He marches at the head of his Storm, the torch in his hands and hundreds of thousands marching behind him. The marching bands drum, roar, and cheer, as an avalanche of flowers greet the soldiers of this revolution. That evening, they no longer need to fight. All that's left to do is to watch the windows of the Reich Chancellery. There, in one window, stands an old man with snow-white hair.[56]

And in another window there is a younger man whose face they have known for a long time. The field marshal and his new Chancellor.

And while endless ranks of the SA are marching past these windows amidst boundless cheers, even the simplest SA-Man knows that all their marching and fighting, all their sacrifice is finally bearing fruit.

This is the moment they have been working towards. They have given their lives for it. They have been faithful and brave.

They wanted their Führer to rise up, so that he could raise up Germany. Now the Führer stands before them as Chancellor and Germany is free.

The SA has ensured its freedom.

And the SA will see to it that Germany will rejoin the ranks of nations with dignity and strength, as their Führer envisioned it.

Among the many songs that evening there is one which they

---

[56] A clear reference to Paul von Hindenburg, the famous Prussian field marshal who led the German Supreme Army Command from 1916 to 1918. In 1925, he was elected President of the Weimar Republic, an office which he would continue to hold until his death in 1934.

couldn't sing with all their heart up till now. But today, on this evening of joy and relief, they can put all their spirit and strength into it.

They fix their gaze on those two men at the window, the old man who represents their people's great past and the young face in which they can already catch a glimpse of their great future...

<table>
<tr><td>

Wir treten zum Beten
Vor Gott den Gerechten,
Er haltet und waltet
Ein strenges Gericht;
Er läßt von den Schlechten
Nicht die Guten knechten,
Sein Name sei gelobet
Er vergißt unser nicht..."[57]

</td><td>

We gather together
To ask the Lord's blessing;
He chastens and hastens
His will to make known.
The wicked oppressing
Now cease from distressing.
Sing praises to His Name;
He forgets not His own.

</td></tr>
</table>

The torch-lit rally in Berlin the evening after
Adolf Hitler had been declared Reich Chancellor.

---

[57] "Dankgebet" by Josef Weyl

The Karl-Liebknecht-Haus during the SA march.

33

Conquest

Now the SA concludes their conquest of Berlin. In a single, concentrated attempt, they storm the bastions and sweep away the occupying forces.

The day of the awakening nation is heralded by the marches of brown battalions, carrying their Standards in a proud and truly glorious display. Swastika flags are waving everywhere.

The last election looms, this ultimate declaration of will, this final confirmation by the German people.

"Gee," says Schulz, "How often have we marched through these streets? I know every little corner around here. Bergmannstraße—Bellealliancestraße—Hallesches Tor—but it all looks very different now, doesn't it? Back then, we always marched against the Commune and now—well, where are they?"

"Where are they?" shouts Ede. "You can seek them all you want. They're gone for life, for all eternity..."

But Schulz only shrugs his shoulders, the eternal sceptic. "We'll see." And he will be right.

On February 27th, a Reichstag night watchman opens a door to the large conference room, puzzled by the slight smell of smoke. He finds himself in front of a raging, crackling, boiling sea of flames.

The Commune has lit its torch. Once again in the dark of night, yet another heroic ambush.

But the brown Germany strikes back. In the blink of an eye, SA-Men have occupied the Karl Liebknecht House. And this Communist headquarters falls despite its concealed alarms, electric door locks, hidden trapdoors, and secret hatches. The sally ports hidden behind wall cupboards and triple-secured, secret corridors could not prevent this.

The SA knows these tricks.

A grinning Schulz enters the secret underground vaults.

"Just like in Boddinstraße!" he growls as he starts to rummage around the place. These vaults are stacked with all kinds of material. There are thousands of letters, instructions, order forms, writings, sketches and also weapons of all kinds lying around. To Schulz this seems like a highly instructive and enjoyable collection.

He fingers thumbs through a bundle of facsimiles. Pushing aside the loosely tied string, he fishes out two or three documents. After reading the first few lines, he straightens out.

"Hermann," he whispers hoarsely, "Hermann, come over here for a second."—And then the two SA-Men sit down on the floor and start reading.

What they are reading are orders from the secret KPD insurgency leadership, directed to their subordinate terror and combat units, dated February 28th, right after the Reichstag fire. They read:

Dear friends!

We have discussed the current situation and agreed on a number of decisions.

1. mass emergency defence in the fight against fascist terror.

2. disarmament of fascist gangs.

3. arming workers and destitute farmers.

4. fraternisation of antifascist police officers with the workers.

5. protest strikes.

Priority has to be given to the expansion towards large-scale self-protection and the establishment of joint patrols with Reichsbanner, SPD, and Christian-Workers. Mobilization methods should be as varied as possible... sirens, horns, whistles, battles, demonstrations...

Schulz whistles through his teeth but says nothing. They take a look at the second sheet, also dated February 28th:

Orders:

1. The combat unit is to be immediately divided into two formations. Comrades with weapons constitute one formation. Comrades without weapons are to be used as couriers.

2. By Saturday, the Reich Courier must be informed about the stock of weapons available in your districts. Carbines, rifles, pistols, hand grenades, possibly machine guns. How much ammunition. Special instruction about explosives.

3. Combat Association, Club, Party, and RMS are to be put on high alert immediately.

4. Deployed auxiliary police officers are to be dealt with by all means necessary, wherever they are encountered. No fascist shall be allowed to cross the street.

5. All strategic Nazi positions are to be identified.

6. Nazis shall receive no mercy.

Highest alert level on Election Day, March 5th, twelve o'clock in the evening.

Arrival of the alarm message. Positive instructions regarding operations within the Reich. Arrival of the Reich Chancellor...

Schulz collects the papers and boots them to the battalion leader, who just takes a brief look inside and immediately rushes off with it. Within that very hour, the communist insurrection orders arrive on Hitler's desk.

And that's not the only thing lying on his desk. There are also Communist instructions for urban warfare, a vile document:

...firearms and explosives are not enough. Chemical agents must be prioritized. Pursuing police officers are to be dealt with using bottles filled with concentrated acid. Thrown against the officer's chest, they will result in immediate incapacitation. The more absorbent the fabric, the more effective the attack. Armored vehicles are to be set on fire by throwing gasoline and benzene bottles, combined with burning rags. The fire is to be nourished by subsequent volleys. Designated throwers are to be distributed throughout the streets. Condensed milk cans are very useful for this. These are also excellent ways to confuse large audiences...

The Commune has thought of everything. Hand grenades, bombs, gas and acid, axes, rope ladders, and crowbars. The Reich capital has been mapped into districts and deployment avenues in exemplary military fashion. Within those maps, each police station and SA home has been carefully marked. So that was the state of affairs right when unsuspecting Berliners strolled up to the ballot boxes.

The next few days are difficult for the SA.

At a surface level, these days are filled with the cheers of the masses, formation of political forces, newspapers writing about the dawn of a new era, nagging, suspecting, deducing—all of them as clueless as ever.

But below the surface, the SA is working in silence. Again and again, the SA is doing its duty.

The SA has conquered Berlin.

Now it must set to cleaning up Berlin. There are rats lurking in their holes, still waiting, still hopeful. They must be burned out.

And that is just what the SA does.

A week later, it is all over.

The process has not been completely quiet. There have been shootings and beatings, some turmoil and even some deaths. But the SA prevented two things: widespread rioting and a full-on revolution.

Partisans of the red revolt are locked up behind the barbed wire of concentration camps. The Reich is saved.

* * *

March and April have passed.

The SA has prevailed against tremendous hardships. No oak wreath adorns the brown cap. No flowers gleam on the brown shirts. But great honor awaits them. Before, they marched alone, fought and won alone. Now millions are marching, the whole of German Berlin. Man by man, woman by woman, and children, boys and girls. Ministers are marching with workers, masters with apprentices, students with the unemployed. And for a whole day the asphalt of this metropolis is steaming under the stride of the people.

The city has turned into a sea of flags! One and a half million people on the Tempelhof fields! They are here because it is May 1st, the day when German workers complete the march into their fatherland! The proletariat of Berlin has stepped forward, and the SA is returning to them what until now they had only possessed in dreams: dignity, simple human dignity.

As the headlights now play brightly over Schulz's face, his high, beautiful forehead gleams, his face becomes free and clear... Does he remember that day in 1926, on Potsdamer Straße?

Does he remember speaking those fateful words: "The worker is a human being too. He's not supposed to be that prole, which the lofty citizens make him out to be. And as long as that hasn't ended, hasn't changed..."

Does the worker Schulz think about it at all?

Now that day has come. All the blood, the comrades they lost—their sacrifices have not been in vain. The SA has won the Reich for the German worker, they have conquered the fatherland for him, the outcast, the lawless, the Fourth Estate. Be proud, SA! Finally the conquest of Berlin is complete.

* * *

That day, the people from Storm 24, Schulz and his men, are sitting together late into the night.

As the morning dawns, Schulz rises and rolls up his sleeves.

"And now let's get to work, boys! That's the best thing about the Third Reich—finally we can work again! Work... work..."

* * *

Proletarian Schulz...

SA-Man Schulz...

Worker Schulz!

The new Germany salutes you!